DEFENDING HEAVEN

"When Legends Rise"

CHAD NICHOLS

DEFENDING HEAVEN

I

The last ray of sun was about to dip behind the mountains of this God-forsaken place. Most of the world see sunsets to be peaceful, but not here...ohhhhhhh not here.

"Echo1, Echo 1 stand ready", I said across the com. "ECHO 1 AT THE READY" replied my front man. We knew tonight was going to be a long one. There was no moon tonight and we have been picking up heavy chatter the past few days. We had intel that tonight an attack on the base was imminent. We were hoping a massive dust storm was not in the cards seeing is how the wind was already making visibility labored. My team was at the rendezvous point where we were trying to intercept the attackers to prevent penetration to the base. Do not get me wrong the Marines that were on the base were well prepared to unleash hell on whatever came their way, but the base was nestled in a valley with mountains around 3 sides. We wanted to make sure they focused on those mountains in case the enemy flanked us and got a vantage point. Seventeen

Tanks were at the ready to disrupt any, and all advance from the south.............we had the north.

My forward sniper scout came over the com "Chaos this is Echo 3; Chaos come in." " Echo 3 Go for Chaos." I have nine vehicles coming in at 1 o'clock, trucks, two heavies in back with multiple shoulder mounted. Count of approximately 35 or so hostile over. Echo 3 roger that on nine trucks at 1 o'clock, trucks, with two heavies and multiple rockets. Echo 1 you copy?" copy that Chaos on your command." "Chaos, Echo 3" "Go Echo 3".... we now have twelve trucks; I repeat twelve trucks. They are stopping at approximately 700 yards, standby."

We were about a mile out from base posted on two ridges. It was like a funnel for the enemy to come through and we had the vantage point. We had good cover in the rocks and our hummers were poised and ready. We had multiple claymore traps set at every angle. My sniper overwatch (Echo 3) was now actually 500 yards in front of us on a lower ridge. They had what looked like a 45-degree advantage on the enemy, but at that angle, it was also easy to fire up at them. If they engaged, it would give away their position. There were seven of us with our AR's, two saw guns (M249 light machine gun) and both hummers with mounted 50 cals.

"Echo 1, Chaos......Go for Chaos.... with 12 bogies we need the hummers at the ready. We need the 50's." QUIETLY, I said to Sutter. "Roger that," he responded. Sutter then manned the .50 cal along with Mitchell on the other .50 cal. I laid down the com to look through my scope.......................

CLACK......CLACK......................CLACK!!!!!   If there ever was a more distinct sound, I do not know it.

"MORTARS....MORTARS," I yelled, GET DOWN!!! We had been made. BOOOOOOOOM ......the mortars were dropping with small arms fire and muzzle flashes in our direction. The attackers were just spraying the mountains with bullets at this point. They have not pinpointed us, but it would not be long. CLACK...........................CLACK!!!! "INCOMING," I screamed!!!!! "ENGAGE....ENGAGE!!!!!" Rounds were hitting all around us. We opened fire which compromised our position. We were taking fire, but not effective fire. We still had the vantage, but we needed to find the guys with the rockets. Jacob was locked in on one truck with shoulder-mounted rockets keeping them at bay. I could see Echo 3 engage which gave his position away and one of the bogie trucks started in his direction. "COVER ECHO 3!!!!!!" ECHO 1 was engaging the 50 and another distinctive sound if you were ever in a firefight was the sound of a 50-caliber machine gun......we called it the Rainmaker!!!! I could see tracer round flying across the desert floor as both sides were heavy in battle. I saw a burst of flames ...... "ROCKET" I yelled! BOOOOOOOOOOOOOOOOOOOM an explosion too close for comfort. Rock debris showered us. I knew we had to eliminate that threat, or we would all be dead.

Suddenly I felt two hammer blows to the chest. I was hit as my body was propelled backward. "IM HIT, IM HIT," I could barely talk from it knocking the wind out of me. Jacob came over to me and checked me. "IN THE VEST HE YELLED... YOU TOOK 2 IN THE VEST" as he pulled me up to cover behind the rocks. "FIND THE ROCKETS... TAKE THEM OUT" I said, as I tried to get my wind back in me!!!! I engaged again, as I could hear rounds zipping past my head.

"CHAOS, MUERTA IS ENROUTE....we are ETA 2 min!!!" (Muerta was one tank from the base unit) "Muerta take a 3 o'clock position east of the right ridge, taking rocket, small arms, and mortar fire, over!!!" I could hear the tanks on the base defending the mountains behind them. We were under attack from all sides–but knew the tanks would clear the threat on base............it was the rockets and mortars that were the problem.

"Muerta, ECHO 3 (I could hear Echo 3 on the com). Go for Muerta," Echo 3 called out "AIM....432N BY 13E FIRE FIRE FIRE"!!!!! He was giving the coordinates of the bogies. Good thing our tanks and marines were lethal and lethal at full speed, and they were about to prove their worth. Echo 1 landed effective fire on the bogie that locked in on Echo 3 and I could see the explosion of the vehicle. BOOOOM.......BOOOM ...... BOOOOM......I could hear the report of our tanks behind us and the shells screamed as they flew over our heads. 2 BOGIES EXPLODED...... "YEA," I screamed....... "Echo 1 you have one coming in hot." One bogie was at full speed coming right at us......it only means one thing, Explosives!!!! "EVERYONE ON THE FORWARD VEHICLE....TAYLOR...DOWN RANGE."(Taylor had a saw and I wanted him to lay suppressive fire on the other bogies behind the speeding vehicle)...... and all weapons unleashed hell knowing if we did not stop him depending on his payload we could die.

I could see the glow of the barrel from the rainmaker as Echo 1 unleashed about 500 rounds per minute along with 4 other guys locked on target. Just a little bit more and that truck would be in Claymore Valley. 3,2....1 and I hit the button. The truck exploded approximately 60 yards out. Shrapnel goes *everywhere. As we ducked behind the rocks for cover the explosion was effective and blew me and Jaker back about 20 feet. It was like a fireworks factory just went up. I looked at Jaker and yelled "KID......KID...... "He was just lying there. As I grabbed his vest, his eyes opened, and he just smiled and gave me a thumbs up from his back in the dirt.*

One bogie left and he was high tailing it out. I could hear ECHO 3 still firing rounds at him through his sniper rifle as he was leaving. "CLEAR YOUR AREA" I barked wanting my guys to make sure that no one had gotten in behind them for an easy shot. I got on the com and requested "DAMAGE REPORT." "ECHO 1 GOOD TO GO." "ECHO 3 GOOD TO GO BUT STILL HAS ITCHY TRIGGER FINGER" (as I heard him laugh before disengaging the com). "RALLY UP," I said in a stern voice (not out of anger but adrenaline).

Just then over the com, I hear damage control. It was the base and part of it was on fire. The mountains were ablaze from the shelling and Echo 1 came up in a hurry with the hummer and said, "GET IN" ….me and the kid hopped in "GO, GO, GO" I yelled. Taylor took the other hummer to grab Echo 3 and we headed to the base to engage. Muerta turned the turret and began to fire at the remaining enemy that was pulling back as we approached the gates!!! The hummers came to a sliding stop as we jumped out with weapons up ready to take out anything that moved. Sutter was engaging the 50 cal and spraying the mountainside in hopes to find any stragglers that might have been hiding. Once we cleared the scene, I yelled, "everyone good?" and as sailors do, I hear "'GOOD TO GO SHEP."

The shelling stopped from all but two tanks that were pushing the enemy back away as they high tailed it out. The commander of the base met me halfway to the briefing tent. "Report," he said. "All accounted for sir, we will debrief in the com room." And that is when he told me that we lost five from mortars. Five good men, five marines that fought for people they did not even know. They fought for the ones that cannot protect themselves. My heart dropped and all I could think about was their families. The fire crew was getting the last two fires under control as I slowly scanned the base. I could see the proudness of these Marines, as they should be, but I could also see their grief for the fallen because this was their family...........and it always will be until they die.

"Team......debrief in 10 in the Com room. Check your gear." I went to thank Muerta the tank crew for breaking from the base under the commander's orders to back us up. I shook their hands and gave them a hug. You guys are second best as I smiled and laughed. They laughed too knowing that sailors and marines ALWAYS razzed each other on who was the best. It was good for us. It helped us keep our edge. But, let there be no doubt. If I were not in the teams, I would be a Marine!!!

I walked into our debrief tent with my team already inside and checking gear. They all stopped and looked at me. I stared at each, and every one of them as I scanned the room slowly. "Good job gentlemen." "HOOYAH" rang out almost in sequence. Check your gear and each other. Make sure we are good and ready to go when needed. I stepped back to my bunk and grabbed some water. I looked at my guys and thought of the five marines that were lost tonight. I know that if I lost one of them, it would kill me. This was my family, my brothers. It was my job to protect them and although they to protect me, I was the team leader. We all gave intel and I hopefully inspired leadership, but if anything bad happened....it was a circumstance I never wanted to face.

Seven guys on the team total and every one of them was exceptional in their position, and exceptional as humans.

Brian Sutter.... this guy was my second in command. He was a big guy. We both came to the same boot camp together when we joined the navy and we both were in the same BUDS class. He would tell me to quit every day and that I was not going to make it as a joke, but would fire us up as a team, and none of us wanted to let him down. It was amazing to see him smiling all the time, and no matter how much the instructors in buds gave him, he smiled and asked for more. An Olympic hopeful in the javelin before he tore his rotator cuff in his shoulder. Do not give this guy a video game to figure out. He is amazing at figuring out patterns to games. This makes him highly effective in the field the way he watches the approach of the enemy. I nicknamed him the man of steel. I trust him with every-thing I have. (Sutter is married and has three girls, two of whom are twins)

Taylor Crowley...... He knows weaponry like he had a gun in his hand since birth. He could handle anything that threw lead downrange from small arms to shoul-der-mounted rockets, and he was dead on balls accurate with every.... single...... piece. This guy would tell you like it is, no matter what your rank, he did not care. If you were screwing the pooch, he would let you know and in a hurry. A leader not only in the teams but in life itself. The men look up to him for his expertise and insight. Former rugby player so he is not afraid to take a hit or give one at that. He is married with three kids (two girls and one boy) and he is an amazing father.

My sniper team was D.J. Singleton and Tracy Ezzell (EZ)......these two made a great team. They both communicated very well and even what seemed at times to have their own language about an acquired target that only they knew but was funny to listen to. They were great being invisible but great warriors when needed to clear houses and much needed in a firefight. Both were very proficient in weaponry and explosives. Singleton is a single guy and EZ is married with two kids. You would swear they are married to each other, how they are so in sync with the task at hand.

Big Mitch.........Michael Mitchell carried the saw most of the time and just loved watching his targets explode under such heavy fire. Big kid, but a true protector and teddy bear when it came to his family, one boy and one girl at home with his wife. He gave up a professional baseball contract to be in the teams......WHO DOES THAT? I am honored to have him with us.

The Kid..........Jacob. He is the youngest on the team and a lady's man. Dark long curly hair when he grows it out with big thick eyebrows. When we are not in the zert and back home off base, the women go W...I....L...D over this kid. Jacob is a special one, wears his heart on his sleeve, and really cares about humans but LEAVE NO DOUBT, he will make evil pay when deserved.

Then there is me, they call me Shepard. It is fitting to a point that I care for these guys like they are my brothers or my kids or rather "my flock." I am married with a beautiful wife and young 3-year-old daughter at home that I miss with all my heart. Without the navy, I do not know where I would have ended up. I am lucky to have this team and would die for anyone of them............twice.

"GET SOME REST," I barked. Make sure you are fresh; we do not know when the next time will come. I got up and walked out of the tent. I swung the canopy door open and scanned the base. In the distance, I saw something staring at me. I say something because it looked human but too tall and large to be human. I stepped forward, one step then two. I wanted to know what this was. I had my hand on my side arm and unholstered it. I came to a trot as to see if would run. It did not. At about thirty yards, I could see it staring right at me. As I got closer, I watched it step behind a vehicle. I ran faster approached the vehicle in caution and raised my weapon to get on target as I came around. It was gone. I looked around quickly to find it. It was gone. I immediately looked around to make sure nobody was watching me as I holstered my weapon. I rubbed my eyes and my face, then rested my hands on my head as I turned around in disbelief. Was I delusional? Am I seeing things? I bent over and rested my hands on my knees somewhat laughing at myself staring at the dirt below me. I got my wits about me quickly. I stood tall and laughed out loud thinking I am going hysterical. I could not lose control of me and put this team in danger. I needed to sleep. I headed back to my tent so I could get some rest. I needed to recoup.

II

The moment the sun's rays pierced the dusty sky the next day you could hear the Marines doing their physical training. We usually join in with these guys for a good warm-up for the day, but we were up early working on the hummers, making sure they were in tip-top shape for the next run. Midday came and some of the guys were working out and some reading trying to escape in any way from this. Do not get me wrong, we all joined the teams to make this world safer and rid it of evil.

We are born protectors, warriors from birth per se, and it is our calling. Any chance we got to call home or imagine being away from here, we took it.

I looked over at the hummer and The Kid was sitting on the hood just looking out into the zert. I got two bottles of water from the cooler and walked over to him. I said "hey kid" as he looked, I had already tossed the water bottle and he just watched it fly right by. It went right passed him and landed 10 feet in the dirt. I just laughed and held my hands up like WTF?? He laughed as I gave him mine and picked up the errant throw that could have been caught mind you. I crawled up on the hood with him and said, "You good?" He said, "yea Shep I am good (in his slight southern draw), just thinking of different stuff." I said, "want to share?" He shook his head silently as he hung his head and then said, "how is it that we as humans get to say when others die." I said, "I don't follow." He looked at me and said, "Humans. We are natural protectors, it is in our DNA, it is in our blood. We seek out those that do harm to others but, (as he hesitated), we do it in the arena of war, and although graphic in detail we do it for a purpose. Mostly good, and maybe some.................not so. When we get back to the states there is violence and people playing God because of drugs, territory or just to have power over someone. People use the VERY FREEDOM we provide and have for over 200 years, and then curse the very way we provide that freedom keeping them and their families safe. They use that very freedom to fight to be controlled by a government that does not have their best interest. Then NOT KNOWING that when they lose the fight and the control is in place, they no longer have FREEDOM!!! NONE of it makes sense to me." I sat staring at him and finally said, "that is some deep shit kid. How much do you think about this? I need you clear out here." He said, "Shep, I am clear. I just question humanity." We sat in silence for a good two minutes and Jacob said to me, "Shep?" I said, "yea kid." "Do you believe in God?" Without hesitation, I said, "with all my heart and soul." He said, "I believe in

God. Do you believe God will question what we do here?" I told him this, "kid, I believe we should forgive as it is written. I believe that God puts us in places in life that he needs us. People say, "he tests us." I do not think it is a test of who we are, I believe he knows WHO we are, he made us. I believe it is a test of WHAT we are. There are situations in life that we walk away from. Family and friends do us wrong and we forgive them. Then, there are situations that come, and we must decide if we are going to get our asses kicked or not. God does not want us to get our asses kicked. Example, these guys we are fighting WANT TO KILL US, THEY WANT TO KILL US KID. I do not blame them as humans, it is the way they were taught. It is the ideology THEY BELIEVE TO BE TRUE, but I am not going to forgive them and go about my way. I am going to make sure they do not kill me and mine. "Do you get it?" He said "yea, I get it. I just struggle with stupidity a lot." I said, "that's why I love you kid, and THAT is why you are a team guy and not some college kid hoping for a desk job when they graduate living in his mother's basement." I looked at him for a good 20 seconds as we sat in silence. "YOU GOOD?" I asked him. He looked at me and said, "I am perfect" with that Jacob smile. I laughed and said, "yes you are kid, yes you are!!!!! Brief in 30." I got a quiet Hooyah as I walked by him slapping him on the shoulder. As I walked past, he said "Shep?" I said, "yea kid" and he looked at me and said, "Thank you." I walked about 20 paces and stopped to look back, "good kid" I muttered as I turned. I walked over to the gym that was an outside type of gym with some weights that were brought, but also stuff like big tires that we sledge and flip. Whatever we can do to stay in shape and keep our bodies sharp. One thing SEALS are is active, and we do not sit still. We have a purpose. We do our job with a purpose; we talk and walk with a purpose. Nothing we do is just dilly dally shit.... it all leads to accomplishing something. I saw the guys and I stopped to finish my water. As I downed my water raising my eyes to the sky to get the last drop. I dropped my head and crushed my bottle, THERE IT WAS. The thing I chased in the motor pool yesterday was standing right in the middle of my guys. I went for my weapon and thought twice. I stared at it and looked at every detail. I was shielding my eyes from the sun that was directly behind it. Approximately 12 feet tall, a huge creature, that looked human. I stared at it and it stared back at me with wondering eyes. My men would think I am crazy if I pulled my weapon and WHY WERE THEY NOT SEEING IT TOO? Is this really happening? I stepped to it to only get closer as it stepped to me tilting its head in wonder like it was trying to figure me out. I heard a whisper that said "you are needed" but nobody and NOTHING said a word. "SHEP, ...SHEP," I could hear Sutter calling my name, but I was unable to look away. "SHEPARD," he yelled. I looked at him quickly and as I looked back, IT WAS GONE!!!

"SUTTER," I yelled out of frustration. He came to me at a trot. Shep you ok? I rubbed my face and tried to clear my eyes. I looked at Sutter in a dazed like state. He said Shep? I said, did you need me? Sutter said, "Naw Shep...we are good." It was not him that needed me.

The Base sirens sounded, and I saw marines scrambling. I gave the order "GEAR UP, GET IN THE FIGHT." I saw a team of medics rushing to the motor pool. The rest of my team went for their gear. Sutter came by my side as we scanned the base and the mountain tops. I heard it again "you are needed." I looked at Sutter and he did not say a word. Two marines were running to me with a purpose and they said, "sir, sir...............you are needed!" Chills overcame my body. "KID" I yelled. "Has anyone seen the kid?" "SIR," one marine said sternly, "I know where he is." He turned to run, and I followed with Sutter on my six. As we turned behind the hummers, I saw the medics working on someone. I stopped in my tracks. I heard them yelling "YOU ARE NOT GOING OUT THIS WAY BROTHER........ CMON.......BREATHE........ BREATHE DAMNIT!!!!" I looked over and saw a rope that had been made into a noose. "NOOOOOOOOOOOOOOOOO," I screamed as I ran over to them. It was him. "CMON," I heard the medic's yell. They were working him hard. Sutter was holding me back so I could let them work. I yelled "CMON KID......CMON!!!!!" I saw them slow and I yelled "DON'T STOP...SAVE HIM!!!!!" They charged the Defibrillator and yelled "CLEAR!!!!" I saw his body lunge. Nothing happened. "CLEAR" he yelled again and all you could hear was one long tone. One doc then stood up sweaty and out of breath and said, "he's gone." He looked at his watch, then at me, and then looked to the ground. I felt Sutter's hand on my shoulder squeeze as I stared in disbelief. Our conversation not 10 minutes ago scene by scene, word by word went through my head. "Shep, do you believe in God?" "Do you believe he will question what we do here?" "Clear out," Sutter barked.... "Clear out," he was barking orders to everyone standing around. I approached Jacob. His eyes still open as I knelt beside him. I grabbed his collar in anger and said "why? Why kid........... WHYYYYYYYYYYYYYYYYYYYYYYYYYYYY" I screamed as I pulled him to me and held him. He was obviously in more pain than anyone knew and did not know how to get help or talk to anyone. I cried as I held him. This was my guy, my team, MY RESPONSIBILITY and I did not listen. I did not spend more time. A MILLION THOUGHTS were going through my head. How could I have saved him? How could I have not seen this? As close as this team was, we all missed this. The doc came and said we need to take him to medical. I felt Sutter's hand grab my collar and go to pull me up as I shrugged him off violently. I stood slowly and wiped my face, slung my rifle over my back. I reached down, gently picked Jacob up from the ground, and cradled him in my arms. "I'll carry him, he is my brother." I stood staring at the heavens for a quick minute as every step I took was heavy with grief with him in my arms. I laid him in the medical tent for the doctors to do their job. With a million questions still going through my mind, "why" ...was the biggest one. I just stared at his lifeless body as he lay on the gurney. The doctor stared at me not moving as if to give me time until I gave him the go-ahead to proceed. I looked at him then back at Jacob, rubbed my eyes, nodded my head and said, "gently doc." I turned back and walked briskly toward our tent. My guys were in a group as I approached, I barked

"WHO KNEW ABOUT THIS".... WHO KNEW HE WAS OFF AND NEEDED HELP MIKE? DJ? WHO KNEW?" Sutter said "Shep......no one knew. Some people hide the pain, and no one knows. You know we would have said something." I dropped my head and wiped my eyes, "you are needed" I repeated, but I was too late.

I sat in disbelief for hours. What went wrong? Why didn't I see something going on in his head, in his questions? How could someone hurt so much to think THIS was a better decision. How can we as humans justify taking our own lives, and better yet, how can we justify taking others? Maybe this is what Jacob was torn about, maybe he ....SHIT who knows. Maybe this and maybe that. We can only guess now because we cannot ask him. The confusion was setting in as if I had scrambled eggs for brains. It was all running together, and I needed to get a grip.

III

My guys sat checking gear as I filled out a report. All was silent, except for the occasional cycling of their rifle chambers. All I could think about was our conversation. When I grew up, I was made to believe that God does not forgive suicide. I do not believe that…of course, I do not know if it is true or not and may never get to know with all my sins in my life. I have had plenty………. but I do believe God is a forgiving God and he knows our pain. I cannot see him turn the troubled away especially when they are good humans. I do not know the answer. I cannot tell you if he goes to heaven or hell. I wish I could answer this for him and me. I wish I could have seen inside his pain. I do not know how to word this in my report and I damn sure do not know how I am going to tell his mother Lisa.

In all the confusion I called my wife. We had a secure connection that was encrypted as to not give our position away, but also not give away our families. The phone was ringing, and my wife answered. I was silent as she said hello.............. again, hello? Shep? She sat silent for a few seconds and quietly said, "talk to me." Tears rolled down my face as I said, "I love you." She gasped and sighed at the same time and said, "I love you. What happened?" "We lost Jacob," I told her. She was silent and said, "how." I said, "not in battle, but by his own hand." She said, "oh my God Shep; what happened?" I told her, "I don't know; he was fighting demons the same time he was fighting for us. Both fights were for freedom............one from tyranny, and one from his own mind. I don't know baby" as I wiped my face in frustration. "I'm sorry" came from my wife's voice. I said, "how's Gesa?" She is a handful and needs her father home. Gesa is my 3-year-old daughter. We had complications getting pregnant for years and were finally blessed with this energetic bundle of sass. Gesa means "strength of the spear." I am not only going to raise her to be fierce but to protect like her daddy. I love her with everything in my being and cannot wait to see her again. She does not know me too well, being that I have been deployed two years of her three-year life, but this is my final deployment, and will make it up to her for sure. As I finished the conversation with my wife, I told her I loved and missed her and to kiss our daughter for me. I will be home soon baby, I love you. And she said, "very much" and I repeated "very much" and that was our way to say goodbye.

I cut the line and sat for a moment collecting myself. I stood up quickly as if to shake it all off. In my report, I requested we accompany our sailor home. It would only be right so I could be there with his mother and make sure all was taken care of. In doing so another team would take our place, but we can come back to the fight once he is laid to rest. I strongly advised permission.

As I walked out of the tent, I noticed my team had taken Jacobs gear and prepared his tribute of the fallen soldier. I hesitated as I stared at the symbol of loss. How could my loss be greater than the five marines we lost just a day ago? How could my grief be more than theirs? They say humans are not affected by death or disease until its personal…. until it happens to them. Then and only then, does it take a priority in their life.

My guys mustered around my back and I felt Sutter and Taylor's hands on each of my shoulders. I turned to them and with a stern voice said, "we finish what we started for Jaker. We hold our heads high for him and show courage. IS THAT UNDERSTOOD," I barked? HOOYAH the guys yelled as if to send a signal to Jacob, and I bet we did. As the guys turned to get some rest, I scanned the base and I spoke very quietly to Jaker…… "kid, I do believe in God and if no one forgives you…………I do! I will see you soon. But not yet…………………not yet!!!!"

I wiped my eyes and THERE IT WAS …. THE GIANT!!!! All I could say was "son of a bitch" as it stared at me and its head twisted like a dog that hears a whistle as if it was trying to still figure me out. I was at a loss. I could not even speak. I stared back with almost the same kind of look; I am sure. This was not my imagination, or was it? It could not be. It got closer and closer to me and as I took a good look, I saw it was a man with armor. A Gladiator of sort and it did not walk, it hovered closer and it stopped about three feet from me. I was in awe. He carried a sword, but unlike any sword I have ever seen. Not straight, but wavy with a two-sided blade as if to rip the soul from you if it were to be thrust into your body. "YOU ARE NEEDED" I heard again. Again…no one and nothing said a word. I was speechless…. I tried to talk. I tried to ask but could not. I tried to move but was frozen.

Again…… "you are needed." With that two massive wings came from behind his back and spread for what seemed like days. The brightest light I had ever seen came from behind him, blinding me to where I could only see a silhouette of him, and he and the light disappeared at the same time.

As if I was in a dream, I heard retreat muffled in the background and it got louder and louder. I shook my head stood at attention as they lowered the Flag for the night. What did I just witness? I still was not convinced I was not dreaming. But If I saw what I thought I saw…………. Why me?

IV

Morning came to a glow over the mountains. In some strange way, this place was amazing and had so much beauty, but with so much evil and death, I just wanted to get out. I wanted it over, win the battle, and get our men and women home with their families. I met with the Team LC that was taking our place so we could accompany our sailor home. Lieutenant Commander Gunner Bezrutczyk (Bez-rut-check) oversaw the new team. Bezrutczyk was an old salt that had 18 years in the teams. He did all from BUDS training to being part of four different teams. He is one of those guys that no matter how bad you think you are; you would have to think twice just to think twice about taking him on. Bezrutczyk met with me in front of Jacobs's fallen soldier tribute. "It's a hard day when we lose a sailor and even harder when we lose a Teammate," he said. "You did your job Shep," as I shook my head. "YOU DID YOUR JOB" he reiterated with more intensity. "I question that sir," I told him. "How could I lead a team and not know the demons inside?" He grabbed me by the back of my neck and pulled me close to his face and he said very sternly "YOU ARE NOT GOD......only he knows all so get over it and get back in the fight." I hesitated and then said, "yes sir." He released his grasp and said, "see you in a few days" and I said, "it better be all of you," with a shit-eating grin on my face. As he walked away, I heard a muffled "Hooyah."

As we turned toward the plane, we noticed the whole base waiting in no particular formation. I stood in awe and saw Muerta (the marine tank unit that broke from base to back us up two nights prior). I stared at him and he held four fingers up across his chest (code 4....stay safe) I grinned. We approached Jacob's casket draped in OLD GLORY. A site you never want to see unless of a veteran that died of natural causes for honor at their funeral. Three on each side grasped the handles, I walked behind. As we lifted Jacob to carry him aboard everyone came to attention. One snap is all you heard. Over 100 men and women come to attention with one noise so distinct it could only be Marines. SAAAALUTE was called and in one motion they gave honor to Jacob. We walked slowly boarding the aircraft making sure giving him the honor he so truly deserves. TAPS playing in the background and a twenty-one-gun salute in the distance. We are all family here. No matter what branch of service we may gig each other about who is the best, but when it comes to honoring the fallen......we do it together as one.

We strapped our sailor down and strapped in. We were in a C130 gunship. The gunship is a troop and supply carrier, but very, very heavily armed. We had to get to altitude fast, so we knew there was a good chance we would have company. The Air force was laying cover on the flight path that we were going to take and all guns on this vessel would be blazing for the first few thousand feet. As the loading ramp came up, I heard the captain say over the com "strap in boys, this is going to be one for the books." Sutter and Taylor took the side guns keeping them loaded with ammo in honor of Jacob; making sure they could take out a few more for him before he left. You could hear the 16's flying over "we have the lead, GODSPEED" came over the com from the Air force. With that…. we were air born. We were heading to Germany to catch a hop on a bigger aircraft (C-17). We were all resting in what might be the worst jump seats ever made. Some of the guys had even unstrapped and laid on the cold hard metal deck because it was better than these damn seats. About an hour in the captain of the plane came back to me and said to me, "sir, you have to see this" and motioned me up to the cockpit. I looked at my guys, unbuckled, and followed him forward. As I got into the cockpit my mouth dropped and my eyes about came out of my head. I was looking out the forward glass and there were HUNDREDS of them. Giants…. GLADIATORS with wings in the lead of our plane almost in wedge formation like you would see ducks flying. Every one of them chiseled as if they were Greek Gods. Every one of them looked as if they were made to fight and protect. I looked at the pilots and said "you see them? YOU CAN SEE THEM!!!" As my voice got more excited. The Captain then said "yes…it's the strangest cloud formation we have ever seen, but whatever it is, it is making like we are flying on ice and we are almost to limit in speed. It's like there is no resistance." I could do nothing but stare at the captain and out the window. The same Giant I saw in the zert hovered in front of the aircraft and looked right at me, "you are needed," I heard again. He then looked confused as he looked at his hand and held up four fingers across his chest just like Muerta did on base as if he were trying to talk to me from what he saw. He then turned and took the lead position guiding the aircraft. The captain turned to me and said "sir......sir, are you ok?" I looked at him for what seemed like a day but was probably more like 10 seconds and turned and walked back to my seat. DJ met me halfway back and asked, "Is everything ok?" I told him yes as I walked by him and said, "some weather pattern is guiding us through the rough stuff." He was like, "hell yes, I love smooth flights." I strapped back in and stared at the flag-draped coffin as I heard over and over in my head "you are needed." I started to question my senses and my senility. What was this? Who was this? and why me?

V

My request was that no letter be sent yet by the U.S. Navy about Jacob's death to his parents. I wanted to be the one to tell his mother and his father. I, wanted them to hear it from us, his brothers, his team, his military family. We landed at Tinker Airforce base in Oklahoma City. I have friends here in the Tacamo Squadron VQ-4 (the Shadows) and were met by the commanding officers of both VQ-3 (the Ironmen) and VQ-4(the Shadows). Both fine squadrons that relentlessly and quietly keep us safe 24hrs a day. Their mission is a top-secret one and their crew in both squadrons are highly trained and are the best of the best at what they do. Commander Aubrey Barrett (VQ-4) and Commander Victor Cook (VQ-3) both met us on the tarmac where the SUV's were waiting. "Shep, (Commander Barrett shook my hand) great to see you again but under these circumstances, I wish you weren't here. I told her this was a trip I did not want to take. I turned to Commander Cook (who was a classic car guy like me) and said,

"Commander how is that 69 Charger running these days?" as I shook his hand. He said "I have no words that can express my sorrow. I'm glad you are safe." I said, "thank you, sir." I said to Commander Barrett, "do you still have that plane that is haunted?" She looked at me and said, "from your lips to God's ears Shep." I chuckled because everyone that had anything to do with VQ-4 knew about "THAT BOEING 707" and the ghost of "Chris Chuck" and his everlasting hold on it. We turned to see them unloading Jacob and stood in silence. We watched as they loaded him into the convoy. I turned and said "Commanders.... I am honored you would meet us here at the plane. Please tell your crews that they are the best of the best for me and I'm proud of all they do." Commander Barrett said, "will do. Tell your men to stay in the fight.... we need you guys." "Aye aye ma'am." I snapped to attention, saluted them as they saluted me back. I shook both of their hands and told them "next time I'm here, beer is on me." They smiled and Commander Cook said, "not only will I hold you to it, we will go for a ride in the Charger. Tell your family we said hey and be good," and with that I barked to my team "MOUNT UP." I joined my men and we had an escort off the base.

I had written a few things down that I might say to Jacob's parents, but I am not a script guy. I will have to just go with it when I see them. I had an hour to think about it. We sat in silence for the most part as we drove to Jacob's home with the occasional relay of intel that we were getting from the zert.

Two right turns and we would be there. My stomach started to feel unsettled. As we pulled up to his home, three black SUV's in a row, Six Sailors in dress whites getting out of all of them. Our uniforms pressed with tight creases; shoes polished like we were going to the Navy Ball. Our Medals in order properly placed on our chest and above all that............THE TRIDENT. The symbol of the Navy Special Warfare Sailors. The Navy Silent operators. Sea Air and Land......The Navy Seals. I slowly stepped out of the vehicle and placed my cover on my head. I could see the neighbor stop cutting the grass as we stood across the street. I said "brothers......help me through this, they are going to need us to be strong." A muffled "Hooyah" came from them. I took three steps and Jacob's mother appeared from the front door. Anxiously scanning the crew looking with a smile on her face for her boy. The smile turned to calm and the calm to desperation. She tried to look over us into the vehicles to no avail. She stopped as I walked to her. The look on my face told the story she did not want to hear. Her hand covered her mouth as I saw her buckle and I caught her before she fell to her knees. Slow tears came from her eyes as she looked at me. She screamed "tell me......TELL ME!!!! TELL ME HE'S OK." I just looked at her with a blank stare and burning pain in my heart. Just then Jacob's father came out and saw the commotion....he took the first step off the porch, grabbed the banister, and slowly sat down. Holding his heart, two of my guys went to him and knelt by his side. He said, "my boy? Where is Jacob?" He then started to sob with no control. His mother was wailing, and the neighbors started to gather. Wives from next door came over to hold Jacob's mother. They walked her into the house as I followed. I looked at Sutter who was with Jacob's father and he nodded his head as to tell me "I'll take care of this" and I nodded back. As I entered the home, I slowly removed my cover. I saw family pictures of Jacob as a kid and graduation from bootcamp. I saw his high school football and baseball pictures too. They were proud of him and he was a spitting image of his mother. She sat sobbing in her chair. I knelt close to her and held her hand. I gently placed Jacob's Trident in her hand and said "I cannot tell you that I have ever felt your pain, nor do I ever want to. I cannot say or do anything to make it subside, only time and prayer will accomplish this task. I can however say this to you. Your son was an intense warrior for this country. Your son was my brother and one of the greatest humans I have ever known. His pain and his fight are over, and he is at peace now." She looked at me with so many tears I could barely see the color in her eyes. She clenched her eyes tight and said "REJOICE.... for he is in the hands of God." Her lips quivered and her body shook. She stared at me and said, "he looked up to you. He spoke of you often and told me how he hopes to be a leader like you. You do what it takes to bring the rest of your men home to their families." A tear slowly ran down my face as I was speechless. I kissed her on the head and told her the US Navy would be in touch today for the funeral and I would see her there. I gave her my number if she needed us while we were in town, and I slowly stood. I said thank you to the neighbors and walked out of the house. His father met me on the porch, stared at me, and hugged my neck as he sobbed. He said, "you did your job son, come home safe." He then stood at attention and saluted me. I calmly grabbed his hand from his brow and held it on my heart and said, thank you, as I ended the meeting with a firm handshake. My men huddled up and we got back in the trucks and drove back to base.

Our families were flown in to see us, so by the time we got back, they were waiting at the base hotel. As we pulled up you could see the anticipation in both my guys and their families. We hugged and kissed our loved ones and maybe just squeezed them a little tighter today of all days. Gesa ran up to me and screamed "Daaaaaaddy." I scooped her up in my arms and kissed her face maybe 50 times in under 3 seconds....... but who is counting? My wife hugged my neck and said, "I miss you so much." I looked at her in awe...the most beautiful woman I know, and I never wanted to take my eyes off her. "I love you too baby" I responded. My guys were looking at me and I said "go.... go...get out of here," This was their time with their families as well as mine and I wanted them to have as much time as they could. I walked my crew back to the room where there was a table set up with Chinese take-out. One of my favorite foods and Gesa's too. She laughed when she saw how excited I was to see it. I said, "I'm starving. Did you order all of this food Gesa?" She smiled and said, "no daaaaaaaaaddy, I cannot pay for all dis food. Mommy called someone and they brang it for me and you to eat." I smiled as I looked into her eyes and the radiance of her smile was mesmerizing. OH, how I missed that little voice. She gets bigger and more active every time I see her. I looked at my wife and silently mouthed "thank you." She smiled her smile and mouthed back "you are welcome." We sat and talked at the table for about an hour and Gesa asked me all kinds of questions. "Did you bring me a rock? Did you get the bad guy?" They just kept coming one after another as my wife graciously let her get it all out KNOWING she wanted my time just as badly but knew my love for Gesa and that she would be going to bed soon. With my belly stuffed I sat back and patted my tummy as my daughter mimicked what I did and patted hers too. I said, "thanks to the chef." Then she copied me saying "tanks to da Jef." It is amazing to me a father's love for their child. I never knew I could give such love being that my father and I always had a very dysfunctional relationship. I was always having to prove I was enough and just as good as my older brother. It was my driving force for years. A year after my father got diagnosed with cancer, we had a falling out and I never spoke to him again, two years later he passed when he lost that battle. I have never forgiven him and do not think I can. It is hard to understand how a child can love and hate a parent so much. This is one reason I tell Gesa I love her every chance I get and that she is enough and very powerful. I want her to feel the love and strength I did not feel as I grew up. I do not ever want her to not talk to me. As I laid Gesa to bed she said "daaaaaaddy, when coming home?" I told her soon baby. I saw her eyes were heavy and falling asleep. I kissed her forehead long and gently as I stroked her hair. She was asleep. "I love you Gesa." With everything I have I love you and I will never let evil get near you.

I looked over at my wife as she lay on her side watching with her head propped up on her hand. She patted the bedside next to her and said, "is it my turn yet?" I crawled into bed and kissed her long and hard. "I love you baby," I told her. She in turn said, "I love you so much" back to me. She asked how I was, and I told her that I was confused still how I did not see it coming. I questioned my ability as a leader because of it and………she said "stop right there!!! YOU CAN'T HELP EVERYONE and you damn sure do not know what everyone is thinking or the demons they are fighting. You are one of the strongest human beings I know" she said. "You are a valued and proven leader and your men love you. THE NAVY LOVES YOU FOR GOD SAKE" as she laughed. I touched her face as I stared at her and said, "thank you for believing in me and always knocking me around when I doubt." She smiled, tucked her head on my chest with my arm around her and we laid and talked for quite a while about all that her and Gesa have been doing, future plans, and when I come home. It was so nice having her there. She is my rock. I love this woman.

VI

The next day the team met up and debriefed on what we were doing. "Jacobs funeral is tomorrow; you know the dress code. We will be leading the precession, two SUVs in front, one behind. Any questions? After the funeral I will meet with Jacob's parents one more time before we fly back at o'dark. Spend time with your family as much as you can."

You could see the rest in the guy's faces and thankfulness in seeing their families and all around just having a break. The ones that did not have families here just went out and relaxed or stayed in and...............well............... relaxed. But even with this time away, we were all itching to get back in the fight and for me, it would be one last fight before I retired.

Jacob was buried in Oklahoma Veterans Cemetery. As we listened to the Pastor bless the burial, I could not help but think of Jacob's and I's conversation that day. Every word, over and over in my head. What did I miss? I started to think backward if I saw any signs from the past. I scanned all the headstones and thought of how many of these men and women thought of or committed suicide. In the distance there he was……the GIANT. He stared at me and I at him. I watched him as he watched the funeral and every time the pastor would bow his head, so would the Giant. I could not make sense of who and what this was. My head spun as I heard my conversation with Jacob and "you are needed" from the Giant. I was in a fog and did not hear the pastor tell us to pay our last respects to Jacob until Sutter nudged me. I slowly took my Trident from my chest as I approached his casket. I walked up to it and pounded my Trident into the top. The team did the same as I grabbed the Folded Flag. This is customary for teams to do this as respect for a fallen team guy. I knelt in front of Jacob's mother Lisa once again giving my sincere condolences as I handed her son's flag to her. She sobbed barely able to breathe. My lips quivered with her pain, but I bent forward and softly told her that her son was a hero in every aspect of life. That it was an HONOR to fight with him and thanked her for raising an incredible human. With that, I shook Jacob's father's hand with both of mine, my white gloves covering his hands. I turned to the Casket, sternly said "ATTENNNNNTION." My team came to attention and we saluted our fallen. I softly said, "Rest brother……I have the watch" and I lowered my salute. The ride back was solemn as we road in silence. We approached the hotel on the base where our families were waiting and glad to see us back. My daughter Gesa hugged my neck and said, "it ok daaaaaaaddy, God have him." I said, "you think so?" and she nodded her head very deliberately and said, "know so." I kissed her face and she said "Daaaaaaaddy, where your goed eagle?" I told her it was guiding Jacob to heaven. She looked in my eyes with her finger in her mouth and then hugged my neck as if to say, "you did good."

My wife smiled and asked if I was ok. I said, "yes, I feel he has been laid to rest and has no more pain." She clutched my hand with both of hers with her head on my shoulder as we walked to the room. We played card games and board games the hotel had in the rooms for the rest of the day. We ordered food in so I could see as much of my family as I possibly could knowing in a few hours we would be on a plane heading back to the zert.

The time came quickly as I put my bag in the SUV. I saw my guys saying one last goodbye to their loved ones as we had to go. I told my wife I loved her, and she said, "very much" and I then said, "very much." I stared at her hard as if to soak every last breath from her to take it with me until I got back. Every tone of her voice and touch of her skin. I held Gesa as tight as a "daaaaaaaaaddy" could hold his little girl without squeezing the life out of her. I said "Gesa, you know I love you right?" and she said, "love u too daaaaaaaaddy." I kissed her head and cheeks as a tear came down my face. I quickly wiped it away as to show her no weakness. I handed her to her mother, kissed her, and turned to get in the SUV. I rolled the window down to get one last look. With my arm hanging out the door I hit the side of the door twice as to say, "let's go" and we were off.

VII

The Air force had a hop going back over the pond and we would land in Germany in about 12 hours. I have been in contact with the Team that took our place in the zert. I was on the com getting debriefed while we waited for flight check and take off. I was taking notes of the sequence of events that have unraveled since we left so I could in turn brief my men on what we are coming back to if anything. The whole time I sat staring at a picture of my wife and Gesa. I missed them already.

As I was listening to the com, I overheard my men saying that it had been such a clear day, not a cloud in the sky until now. It looked like a storm was brewing. I got up and walked to the aft of the plane and down the loading ramp. I looked up and they were right, it did look like it was about to storm. I stood and watched the clouds swirl and lightening in the distance. I headed back up the ramp and into the cockpit where I asked the pilots how it looks, and are we going to get off the ground before this storm comes in? They told me that we are on ground hold trying to find out where the storm was moving so we could take the right runway. "Shep, we will let you know asap when we know. It shouldn't be long now." I thanked them and walked to the aft of the plane again. The guys were all huddled and pointing at different spots in the sky. "Shep, I have never seen anything like this one," Brian said. Some clouds are going one way and the others going completely opposite." I said "yes, that is strange" in a somewhat puzzled voice. Just then the pilot said, "all aboard, we have a 10 min window to launch. It's going to be close." I told the men "GET STRAPPED IN." We all ran for our seats and raised the ramp. The engines were turning, and the pilot unlocked the brakes. I heard "Alpha One you are clear to taxi runway 3-2, clear taxi 3-2." The pilot responded, "roger taxi 3-2. How are we looking on time?" The tower came back and said. "It will be a rough climb but get to 30000 as fast as you can." The pilot responded, "roger tower hi-performance climb," and you could hear him chuckle. "Hang on boys, we are going to climb fast, I hope you have your barf bags with you." I saw Sutter and Taylor laughing as they looked at me and said "we don't need no stinking barf bags" copying a scene from a famous movie in their own way. DJ looked like a little ADHD kid bouncing up and down in his seat and all I could do is laugh at these clowns and THANK GOD they are on my side. I could hear the engines spool to full throttle, and we were on our way down the runway. Faster and faster and the front wheels lifted, then the back.... we were air born. The plane was thrashing as each wing took its turn diving on one side, then the other. The nose would dip and then head straight up. It felt like an 18-wheeler had hit the side a few times. I felt like something was not right. I unbuckled my belts and started to slowly make my way forward trying to keep my feet. The nose dipped and we were headed to earth or so it seemed. I fell to my ass and slid about halfway down the cargo bay. The nose came back up and I could hear the engines throttle up and down as the pilots fought the storm. The Night sky would light up with all the lightning outside.

I finally made it to the cockpit to ask the pilots if everything was ok. I opened the door and said "gentlemen, do we need to put our chutes on" then I tried to laugh, and I could not as I looked out the front window. THIS WASN'T A STORM...............THIS WAS A BATTLE!!!!! The pilot started to talk, but I heard nothing as I watched thousands upon thousands of Giants guarding our plane. But I could not identify what they were fighting. The images were all black with black wings of a bat. Long pointy fingers with black claws. Their faces, I have never seen so much pain. They looked as if they were screaming for someone to kill them but could not get the noise out of their mouths that were almost held open. Like they were screaming for someone to do anything they could to put them out of their misery. The Giants were bludgeoning them with their swords, but instead of their blood falling to earth..........it went up. It was like a sea of black blood that was suspended above the battle. SUDDENLY...One of the black creatures SLAMMED against the nose of the aircraft and grabbed the front window. You could hear it screaming and looking right at me. I jumped back as my back hit the cockpit door in fear. Its nails were extremely sharp. You could hear the metal being ripped from the plane. Nothing scares me…. but this thing sure did. A Giant came from behind him and thrust his sword into and through the heart of this evil creature. Over and over the Giants would plunge their swords into the heart of these creatures. It seemed like it was the only thing that killed them. They were bouncing off the plane one by one as if they were trying to get into us. The pilot was still talking as his voice rang in my ear in and out of muffled and coherent words. It would go in and out of clarity like I was coming too from a head injury. He was saying it was bad weather and to strap in the jump seat. Why am I the only one to see this? We started to stabilize and less banging on the plane. I watched as Giants guided the plane further and further from this battle, or as it was to the pilot's, "bad weather." I was in awe of what I just saw. I then see "my giant" in the window. He looks battered and tired. He stares at me and slowly nods his head as if to tell me "everything is ok." All I could do is stare at him. I unbuckled my belt and walked back to the guys. Sutter and DJ were laughing, and DJ rang out "WOOOOOOOOOOO what a ride." I said, "damage report" and they all said, "good to go." Big Mike looked at me and raised his barf bag like he was saying "allllllllllmost." Sutter said, "you good Shep?" and I said "Hooyah" in an exceptionally low tone. I sat in my seat buckled up as my stomach felt queasy. I took a deep breath, dizziness came over me as I laid my head back and slowly went to sleep.

VIII

We landed in Germany and had about 4 hours until the next hop to the zert. The only thing about this hop is we had to jump with chutes over the base because this plane was not stopping. While in Germany my mind was going 100mph on what I saw or thought I saw or......whatever. I went to the base church. I found the priest and said, "Father please forgive me, but I need to talk." He said, "are you ok my son" with a thick German accent. I went into the confessional and kneeled. "Forgive me father, for I have sinned, but that is not what this is about. Father, I'm seeing things. Well…I think I am seeing things. Hell, I don't know if I am or if I'm not." He said, "I'm not following you." I said, "I have been seeing figures, GIANTS!!! I can't explain it but" and I suddenly stopped. I started to think that I cannot tell anyone about this…. ANYONE. The father was asking me to tell him what's wrong and I stood up and said, "I'm sorry for wasting your time father, I have to go." I opened the confessional and swiftly walked away.

I yelled back at the priest as he peered out the confessional and said "say a prayer for me father, I need it............. BAD!!!!!"

When I got back to the plane and gathered my guys. "HUDDLE UP" I barked. "Check your chutes and check each others. We are going to have to jump home." These guys lived for this shit. It was just another jump for the team, and they loved coming in silent. Just as I was going to get my chute the Captain of the C17 we hopped from OKC to Germany ran up to me and said. "Shep, can I borrow you a minute"? I said "sure, is everything ok? Do we need the guys?" "No," he said, "nothing like that." He brought me around to the front of the aircraft and pointed at the windshield. I stared at it and put my hands on my head. It looked like a grizzly bear had scratched all the way down the windshield to the nose of the aircraft. He said, "Do you remember any birds during that storm?" All I could think about was that evil black creature grabbing the windshield trying to get to us before the Giant drove his sword into his heart. Staring right at me as it attacked the aircraft. Never taking its eyes off me. I then said, "no... no, I don't remember ANYTHING hitting the aircraft other than rain." "Could it have been lightning?" The pilot then said, "well if it was lightning it would have to be three bolts exactly the same length apart at an angle lightning normally doesn't travel." Then he said, "so.......... probably not." Well, I just wanted to show you and see if you remember anything Shep so I can put it in my report and pass down log. As he walked away to look over the rest of the aircraft I slowly backed away from the craft and saw multiple marks by the doors, windows, and aft ramp. SOMETHING..........was trying to get to us. Something wanted in that plane, and I think "I" was the target.

IX

We checked our chutes and stored them by our seats until ready to take off. Some of the guys were talking about God knows what, but having a good time and laughing hard. They needed this. I believe laughing heals the soul, and in the jobs that we do, we tend to lose a piece of our soul it seems every time we go on a mission. The things we see are horrible and the things we do may be horrible in some eyes but warranted to rid evil out of the very DNA some possess in their bodies. Like I said before, I do not know if I will make it to heaven with the sins that I have been carrying. I believe in justice, but more than not I believe in vengeance and was always taught "vengeance is the Lord's" and that he would punish the evil. For some reason, I thought I should be able to as well. I believe there should be fear in this world of what can happen to you if you take it upon yourself to steal from someone, take advantage of people purposely, or kill someone in cold blood because you either want what they have or you are just a cowardly asshole that likes to terrorize people. I believe the prison system is a joke and do not believe in giving someone a second chance after raping and killing someone's loved ones. People say we need to privatize the prison system due to taxpayer cost and some have done this already. Just remember it then becomes a business, therefore, crime is needed to stay in business. Judges and police officers then become employees on the payroll to ensure that happens. I am getting on a tangent here, but with the time we have before launch my mind goes over anything and everything. I often question what it takes to get to heaven or if I am just as evil as the ones I speak of. I will not know until that time… if there is a judgment or if the decision has already been made once you pass a certain point in sins. Is there a limit on the amount of "sin" that is acceptable? I wish I could talk to those that went to heaven and those that went to hell. What was the deciding factor for your ascension or descension? Is there a gauge on "what sin is a bad one and what is ok?" It would be nice to have this knowledge.

My mind must have wondered for a while. The pilot came to me and said, "wheels up in 30." I stood up and stretched raising my arms straight over my head as high as they could go. I signaled Sutter "up in 30." He then relayed it to the men. We all went into the plane and began to put our chutes on and checking each other and then checking each other again. The base knew we were coming in by chute, so we would not be shot by friendly fire as we landed inside a well-secured fort. I barked "check your gear, check your reserve." We were geared up and in our seats. As the cargo ramp closed and we got the thumbs up on it being secure we started to taxi. This jump is an everyday jump for us, so it should go smoothly. You never know when you have some bad guy staring up at the moon as you cross in front of it and all hell could break loose, and we would be sitting ducks. We have the Marines scanning the mountains with their night vision scopes, but there is always a chance one slips through, and that is the one we must worry about.

My mind was still going 100mph. I was thinking is this my last jump before retirement? What kind of job am I going to do when I get out? What am I going to do with my family when I first get back?" Everything was running through my mind at once. I looked at my guys and all of them had their head either back against the bulkhead or forward resting on their chute. We had about 5 hours before we would jump so it was good they got the rest. Rest was much needed. I stared at the picture of my wife and Gesa. How I missed them and how I could not understand the resilience my wife has had during our marriage with all the being gone and understanding of my job. She is an amazing person. I hope Gesa will one day understand what I was doing and why I was not there, but I will be there to watch her grow, and I will not miss a minute. I will get to see her play sports and go to her proms (and threaten her prom dates). I want to see her grow and become the strong woman I know she is going to be. My heart grows when I think about the time I get to spend with them.

The red light in the cabin came on meaning we are coming up to the jump site. I barked "GENTLEMEN, MAKE READY." We all stood and got the blood moving in our bodies. I said, "radios on all call" (this is so we could hear each other talk without hitting the button or hands-free you might say). Captain came over the com and said "Gentlemen, it's been a pleasure...... GODSPEED." The yellow light came on and I barked "STAAAAAAAAAAND IN THE DOOR," as the aft ramp of the plane lowered. All eyes on me as I held my fist high meaning hold your position. Green light blinked three times...I called out "GREEN GREEN GREEN!" We started to walk to the back with DJ in the lead and Brian to follow. I called out "THIS IS WHAT WE DO" and "HOOYAH" came from my men. DJ did a backflip off the ramp and he was air born. Brian after him, then big mike. Taylor jumped backward saluting me and Ezzell closely behind him. I turned and saluted the flag that was hanging from the airframe and I was out.

It was cold up here, but the temp would go up as we got closer to the zert. It was quiet and there is really nothing like it. The adrenaline that runs through your body no matter how many times you have jumped before, but the utter peace that you feel rushing to earth. It is a love-hate relationship for me. I was above my men watching them and listening to their chatter. "Check your altimeters," I told them. We had night vision goggles on so we too could scan the drop site as we got closer. All was well.

Or so I thought. I caught something out of the corner of my eye. Was it a bird? It could not be a bird, we were still too high. Suddenly I heard a scream and my chute was sliced. I had lost all lift. I was plummeting to the earth. I cut my primary and deployed my emergency chute. Sutter

came over the com and yelled "shep…what happened….
are you ok?" I said, "something cut my chute." He was like
"wtf could it be up here?" Sutter barked "men scan the hills
and the skies." Just then it flew right in front of me. It was
one of the evil black creatures I saw on the plane. As I
drew my handgun, I scanned the skies for the Giant and
there were none. It swooped at me again grabbing for me.
I fired off three rounds. "Sutter….do you see anything flying around me. I have something up here and it is coming
after me." Sutter said, "what are you talking about. I see
you clearly and there is nothing up here." Just then the
lines on my emergency chute were grabbed by this thing as
it held me at a dead stop suspended in the air. It stared at
me with that open mouth and face of pain with its wings
slowly holding its position. I emptied my magazine on it
as I watched it rear its arm back and cut clean through my
lines. I was gone. I was dropping to earth with nothing
to stop me. I tried to fan out flat as I blasted past Sutter.
Sutter screamed, "SHEP!!!!!!" I was tumbling now out of
control…. Sutter had ejected his primary and was now in
a full-speed vertical drop to me coming headfirst. We were
coming up on the earth extremely fast now. I could hear
the guys cussing and telling me to hang on that they are
coming. Two others had cut their primaries and were coming like bullets. I could see DJ pulling his chute toward me
as if to catch me because he was below me. I was coming in
way too hot and I knew if I hit him at this speed it would
kill us both, so I veered from him narrowly missing him.
He called out "you son of a bitch." Sutter was almost to me,
but we were about to earth. I turned to Sutter and motioned

Pull 2 (as I reached across my chest pulling my hand across and holding up two fingers) for him to pull his emergency and he yelled "NOOOOOOOOOOOOOOOOOOO." I motioned again and I saw him pull at the last second as he screamed "NOOOOOOOOOOOOOOOOOO." I gave him a thumbs up and smiled, and a peace that I have never felt came over me.

"Base 1 Base 1 this is Echo 1 come in damnit. base 1 base 1 this is Echo 1." GO FOR Echo 1. "MAN DOWN, MAN DOWN...WE NEED A HELO AT THIS POSITION. LAUNCH THAT BASTARD NOW...GET HERE GET HERE" Sutter barked!! "CMON MAN BREATHE, BREATHE YOU BASTARD!!!! COVER SHEP...WE MIGHT HAVE COMPANY." Taylor said, "every bone in his body is broken. We need to traque him." Sutter was yelling "fucking c'mon man. Don't you die on me!!!!" "His chest is like pudding," Taylor said. "Base 1 where the fuck is that chopper, we have a man dying here." Sutter got up with his hands on his head. "he said something was up there with him and cut his chute. WHAT THE FUCK COULD BE UP THERE?" Sutter drew his rifle and started firing his weapon frantically in the air yelling, "COME TRY ME MOTHER FUCKER…... COME TRY ME!!!!!" DJ yelled, "CHOPPER CHOPPER" …as he threw a flare. As the chopper was landing, EZ and big Mitch got in a tactical position to cover. Sutter motioned for the board. He got the board and ran over to Shep. "ROLL HIM ON HIS SIDE," Sutter barked as he placed the board under shep. The men picked him up carried him to the chopper and "GO GO GO," Taylor screamed telling the pilot to get out of here. The 7.62mm mini machine guns were showering

the zert in case any unwanted had heard the commotion and laying cover fire as we got altitude. The doctor on board said, "WHAT HAPPENED?" "Both chutes malfunction and shep dropped from about 8000 feet," said Sutter. The doctor said, "he is not breathing and there is no pulse." Sutter lunged at the doc, grabbed him by the collar and yelled, "THEN MAKE ONE!!!!!!!" The doctor was doing everything he could. Taylor hooked up an I.V. and Adrenaline was pumped into Shep. "CMON SHEP.… CMON MAN," big mitch cried out. The chopper was landing on base and the whole medic group was ready to jump into action. They pulled him from the chopper and ran to the medic tent. The whole team had a hand on the stretcher to give an extra push of speed to get shep there. The doc was sitting on the gurney as we pushed straddling shep as he started cutting his chute pack and uniform off. THE LIGHTS FLICKERED. "Do we have a storm coming in?" someone yelled. "Not supposed to," someone answered. THE LIGHTS FLICKERED AGAIN!!!

It is the most surreal thing to watch myself being worked on in the corner of the tent. I had left my body, but I could hear everything and see all the confusion. I heard a BOOM as loud as thunder and a second…. then a third. I went outside the tent to look leaving them to work on me. I stood and watched GIANTS falling from the sky hitting the earth and taking a defensive stance. There were hundreds falling and all you heard was the thundering booms as each Giant hit the earth. What was going on…was I dead? How did this happen and how am I seeing all of this? I looked back in the tent and the doc was cutting my chest open to get to my heart. As he split my ribcage he suddenly stopped, and his head dropped. Sutter pushed one medic out of the way to look. My heart was mush, it had exploded on impact and I was gone. I stood in disbelief as I relived the attack and Sutter cutting his primary chute to save me, putting his life in jeopardy too. Suddenly My GIANT showed up right in front of me and said, "we don't have much time." I could see him talk and hear him. I looked at him in wonder and astonishment. He said, "my name is Raphael we must go." I said, "Go?" What do you mean, "GO?" Raphael looked to the skies and said, "I do not have time to explain but if we do not, we will die." I said, "look over there RAPHAEL, I AM ALREADY DEAD!!!!" He looked at me sternly and said "listen to me, physically you are dead on earth.... your soul is not, but if you don't listen to what I'm saying.........it too will die here today!!!!!" He grabbed my arm as another Giant grabbed the other. I heard screaming in the distance. It was those black things and they were getting closer. Thousands of Giants took a battle stance all with weapons of choice it seemed. Ten Giants surrounded me as if to become an angelic shield. I saw a dome of feathered wings over my head and around me. We lifted as the battle came to the skies. The Giants had formed an impenetrable dome-type fortress around us as we all ascended to the sky. The fighting was fierce, but they never let the black souls get through to me. I asked Raphael, "what do they want and what are they?" He said, "those are the Suhtan (Sa tawn), and they are the tortured souls of the devil. They are the worst of the worst on earth that never had a chance at heaven and went straight to hell." I said, "why are they fighting you,"

Raphael said, "They want you." "Me?" I said. "why me?" They want your soul to bring to the Devil." I calmly said, "well I would appreciate if that didn't happen." As we went higher and higher.... I looked down and could see the tent where my physical body was. I could see Sutter sitting with his hands in his face and the guys in disbelief. I calmly said, "stay the course old friend" and with that Sutter looked to the skies with tears running down his cheeks as if he had heard me. All I could do is stare at him as he dropped from sight.

X

As I watched the earth fade, I suddenly thought "MY WIFE…MY DAUGHTER GESA, I HAVE TO GO BACK I YELLED!!!!!" "That is not possible," Raphael said. "YOU DON'T GET IT RAPHAEL…. I NEED TO SEE MY FAMILY." Raphael stopped our flight and said, "LOOK AROUND YOU…. THESE DEFENDERS ARE FIGHTING FOR YOU. You are needed and it is with us. Your family will be notified by the US NAVY, I am sorry. If we do not get out of here, we will all die, because the Sutahn will not stop until they get you." "Explain why me? Explain why every other time you were there but when that "THING" cut my chute you were not." "We were diverted in a battle that was purposely made by the Sutahn so you would be left alone. As for why you, that will all be explained soon." I hung there in disbelief as tears fell from my face. My wife and daughter do not know what was going on. How is my wife going to get through this and how will I ever live in death not being there for my daughter? We faded into the dark abyss as we ascended into the universe. My world and everything I knew in it was gone and now, just a memory.

There was a silence that was deafening up here. You could not even hear wind go through the wings of these Giants. It was beautiful up here and I am quite sure we were in a part of the universe that scientists have not even thought about seeing yet. The worlds up here were unbelievably beautiful.

There was a kaleidoscope of colors here that I can guarantee have not been created yet on earth. As I took this all in, I could see Raphael look back at me to make sure I was ok as he led the way up. As we got closer to our target, I could see what looked like "brigades" of Angels. We would pass through them and every single one of them was staring at me. We must have passed through seven layers of these brigades and all eyes were on me. I could see all races from young to mid-30's I would say. Some looked battle-hardened and somewhat I would call teenagers. I was in awe and I wanted to wake from this dream but part of me did not. Each Giant had what looked like weapons of choice or better yet different weapons that they were given to fight the Sutahn. I shook my head in hopes to wake now, but it did not work. I shook it again looking to wake up to my team getting ready for battle in the tent back in the zert. No luck. This was not a dream but reality. Now My definition of "reality" was something new. Something I had to learn all over.

As our ascension came to an end, we were met by another Giant. His eyes as blue as the clearest water in the ocean. His hair was long and as white as the color white itself, maybe even whiter. His face very defined with a very stern look and his skin as pale as an albino. He and Raphael seemed to have a heated discussion while each one turned and looked at me during this conversation several times. The new Giant dropped his head in discussed and walked over to me. He was amazing to say the least. His body too was chiseled like Raphael's. He stood about four feet from me and stared down at me as if he were trying to read my soul. He looked up and down at me several times and said, "SPREAD THEM!!!" I said, "did we get pulled over for getting up here to fast?" He did not like my joke and we came nose to nose. He again said, "spread them" in a calm noticeably confident voice. I said, "spread what?" "YOUR WIIIIIIINGS," he exclaimed as he turned from me raising both of his arms in the air. My eyes got as large as hockey pucks and I felt my back twitch and my dome of angels backed away from me as two wings spread from behind me. I heard a gasp and chatter from thousands of defenders. The Giant turned to them and a hush came over them. I looked around as they were pointing at me and some of their mouths wide open. The new Giant looked at my wings in awe and I watched his face as he looked harder and harder at them. He turned me around and said, "how can this be?" He called Raphael over and asked him to look with him. I said, "can you tell me what is going on?" "Do you have a mirror and maybe I can help you look too......for whatever it is that you are looking for." He turned me back around and looked sternly at me. He said, "My name is Gabriel. I have been put in charge of your training." I said, "training for what?" He said, "how to fight. How to protect from evil!!!!!" I said, "I made it to heaven?" Gabriel grabbed my shoulders and got in my face and said "not......even......close." This guy did not like me I could tell. I am a rather good judge of character and this guy did not like me. I am going to have to put in for a transfer to another angel. He had turned and was going to talk to the other angels when I said, "But I'm an angel so that is a good start." He turned back quickly and said "son...... you are no angel. The ones you see here are Defenders, protectors you might say. Raphael and I .... are angels, Arch Angels. You will meet another soon. He over-sees all of Gods Armies." I said, "wait a minute, I died a NAVY SEAL and now you put me in the ARMY??? Nooooooooooooo, this is not ok!!!" Again, he did not like my sense of humor. He started to walk away again, and I said, "I don't belong here. "I belong on earth with my team and my family." He kept walking away. So, I yelled at him, "HEY GABRIELLE" calling him a girl's name. This was prooooooobably not a good idea as I yelled, "I DON'T BELONG HERE!" Once again he turned quickly and you could see him turn red but in a calm voice, he said, "you are right..............you don't; look around you. Do you see them staring at you? They are in disbelief that you are here too." A mirror appeared in front of me as I looked at myself. I touched the mirror as if to reach the person in front of me to make sure I was seeing me. He came up behind me and said, "spread them." I was speechless and as I spread my wings all I saw was black and gray feathers. NOT ONE was white like the others. The others were

"mostly" white with a little black and a little gray. I ……….
had no white…. not one feather. I looked frantically for a
white feather and to my dismay, I could not find any. In
the middle of my back was one lone red feather. As red as
red could be it stood alone dead center. Gabriel then said,
"you see Shep, the darker the feather the greater the sin.
They have never seen someone with so much color in their
wings up here. You are going to have to earn their trust."
I then said, "there is NO WAY I have sinned this much."
Gabriel then said, "you sure about that?" I stood staring at
me in the mirror. I would look at me, then them, then me,
then them. "When I say you should not be here, I meant
it. You made it by one vote. One defender vouched for you
with their own soul. If you prove him wrong, he too will
be brought to the Sutahn along with you." "Who would do
this for me?" I asked. "Why would you fight so hard to get
me when they wanted me too? Why did both of you want
me so badly." Gabriel brought me my weapon. He said,
"you yield the Trident. The Trident you wore on your uniform was a symbol for fighting evil. It was not in the orig-
inal drawing of the artist. It was placed in the drawing by
Michael, the one in charge of God's Armies. He drew it in
one night when the artist was sleeping and when he woke
the next morning, the artist knew it was a gift …. given for
a reason. That one day, he would know the meaning of it.
The Trident is the only weapon that can pierce the heart of
the devil, grab it, and pull it from his very chest. The middle spear is to pierce it as it is plunged deep into the devil's
chest. The outer prongs are barbed "inward" as to grab the
heart where it cannot escape and hold onto it as the owner

of the Trident pulls with all his might to extract the devil's heart. THIS, is why both of us wanted you so badly. Them, to keep you from any chance of capturing the devil's heart. Us, to have a chance of ridding the world of evil. But by the looks of you, our chances are very slim," as he ended his little speech. "Who vouched for me? I want to know," I demanded. "In time," Gabriel said.... in time" as he walked away. "Raphael, get him into training and let him know the rules he barked. And Shep....... WELCOME.... to Defending Heaven."

XI

Raphael said, "come with me so I can explain what we do. What we can, and what we cannot do. There are rules even up here. They are simple in thought, but when your thoughts affect your heart, they are impossible. You must make sure you abide by the rules.

Rule #1.... you cannot go to earth for ANY reason without permission and unless accompanied by us or if we ask you to accompany us.

There is so much evil on earth that if you go alone your chances of being attacked are great. We have lost many that could not control their thoughts of what used to be and have now become lost with the Suhtan. If there is someone chosen as you were. We will go in armies.... not solo."

I asked him, "when I was on earth and saw you and only you. Why were you there alone?" He said, "I am an

Archangel, but the clouds you saw above you on those days were the armies watching for any trouble. Even I do not go to earth alone. If the devil ever got ahold of an Archangel, it would be one of the greatest prizes he could ever get, and his power would grow 100-fold."

"Rule #2……………. Stay in the cleanse no matter what when we cleanse the blood of the evil. Never ever leave. We cannot let a drop of the evils blood fall to earth. This will strengthen and spread evil on earth at a rapid pace."

I asked him, "has a drop ever made it to earth?" He said, "yes…many over the years. We try our best to keep it cleansed, but some escape the funnel and make it to earth. Evil on earth comes in many forms. It could be someone that physically hurts or kills someone else. Someone that mentally hurts someone, and it even comes in the form of making disbelief in facts leading humans to follow falsely a path that is wrong. Your media is exceptionally good at that one," he said. "There are many ways evil works…. we must keep it from growing."

"Rule #3………. We are the last line of defense for Heaven's gates. Protect them and protect each other up here. Fight as you are trained, and we will be victorious."

I said, "that's it? Three rules? That is all you have." Raphael looked at me and said, "do you need me to bring you a mirror again," as he pointed up and down at my wings. "You are "obviously" not the best at following rules."

He then said "as you fight and over time protecting heaven. You will begin to lose the color in your wings and the feathers will turn white. For you, it will be a long time; do not try to count days, months, or even years. It will be impossible for you to keep track. Just do your days… each one and you will someday pay your debt. Time up here goes faster than on earth…. a month here is like a year down there. Remember this because events will come quickly that you will not want to forget. When all your feathers are white, you have earned your way to heaven."

I then said, "you say that as if I'll never get the nod." He looked at me and smiled as he motioned for me to follow. I barked at him "is that a yes or no?" He did not answer.

This is where we will train you to fight. "train me" I said? I know how to fight, and I was taught by the best all over the world. I am a seasoned warrior." Raphael then explained, "yes, on earth you operated with the best of the best and you were a legend. Here it is different, much different. The Suhtan have many layers of evil. As we get closer to the Devil, the evil is harder to figure out. The first two to three layers we encounter fly and move in patterns. They are easy to vanquish. I believe they are pawns and there to tire us out before the real evil tries its hand. When, and if, you ever make it to take the shot at the devil he will have an almost impenetrable dome of the most evil of evil flying around him as a shield. Up, down, side to side and even back and forth. Finding the pattern to each layer of evil is key to get more attempts at the Devil. It will not be easy and has not ever been."

"Am I the only Seal up here?" Raphael laughed and said, "no sir. I will introduce you to your team of defenders. You will know some, others were before your time. We are calling on you to lead this team." I said, "how many are there?" Raphael looked at me with a smile and said, "come.... let us meet your team."

XII

As we walked the skies, Raphael talked to me about the expectations of all of us, and how we must keep evil at bay and never let it make it to Heaven.

We came upon a group of what looked like 100 men. I could only see their backs and they were cheering something. As we came up to them there were two men arm wrestling. We stood looking over their backs as I looked up and down the line at these men. They were hard-looking, but their faces were focused. Raphael said, "Say something, get their attention, and introduce yourself." I then said, "should I interrupt their competition." Raphael said, "A leader doesn't question his own authority."

I looked up and down the line again and said "gentlemen," and no one budged. I cleared my throat with a small cough and said "GENTLEMEN," a little louder and two turned to look at me and looked back at the competition. I looked at Raphael and he just shrugged his shoulders like "is that all you got?" So, I coughed hard, cleared my throat, and yelled at the top of my lungs "HOOOOOO OOOOOOOOOOOYAH!!!!!" EVERY.... SINGLE.... ONE in unison turned toward me and yelled, "HOOYAH, HOOYAH, HOOYAH!!!!" It was the greatest noise I have heard since I died on earth. They stood and stared at me. Each one had the shiniest gold trident in their hands. This was my team, my brigade, my operators, and defenders of Heaven. I walked back and forth looking them up and down. I barked "GENTLEMEN, my name is" ....and I did not even get it out of my mouth and one guy from the back yells "SHEPHARD!!!!!!" They all laughed out loud at this breaking of ranks per se. I said "yes, and who do I have the pleasure?" I saw a path being made and one man was saying "make a path and make it wide, make a path and make it wide." A huge grin came over my face hearing that. It is a term used mostly in NAVY boot camp when one company is about to run through another company that is in the way). A man bigger than life stood in front of me and said "hey Shep do you remember me?" "Remember," I said? "Hell, we are brothers and I have missed you." It was Roberts, one of the greatest Seal snipers in history. "It is good to see you old friend," I told him as I gave him a huge hug. "My name is Shephard, or you can call me Shep," as I turned again to my men. "IT IS MY PLEASURE to be in graces of my fellow operators." As I looked around, I stumbled on my words seeing that all their feathers were not as colorful as mine were. "I am going to ask for your assistance in debriefing me on the tactics you have learned about our enemy and also train me, again (as I looked over at Raphael) on how to best fight with you. I promise you as on earth my oath to you will be the same that I will never...................... NEVER leave you behind."

"HOOYAH," rang out again and it was like hearing church bells as a kid, the beauty of it. Each man took his turn and introduced himself to me and as I came to the end of the men, I saw one man in the distance. His head was down, and I looked hard at him and then looked at Raphael. I said, "Teammate, are you ok?" He stepped forward and as he got closer a tear fell from my eyes. One.... then many. I yelled, "KID? KID IS THAT YOU????" He raised his head and it was Jacob!!!! I YELLED, "JACOB" ...JAKER MY BOY!!!! I KNEW IT.... I KNEWWWWWWWWWWW IT." He gave me a big hug and kept saying he was sorry. I told him to stop and there was nothing to be sorry about. I told him "it is I, that should be saying I'm sorry. I did not know you were battling demons. I should have seen it. I should have been there." He said, "no, you were the only one that kept me from doing it sooner. You saved me until I could not do it anymore." I held him close and looked at his face. "It was you," I said. "You are the one vote that got me up here, weren't you?" He smiled and nodded his head. Then his face went serious and he told me "do not screw this up, because if they send you down, I have to go with you and that won't be good for you!!!" I stared at him and said, "I've been so warned" with a grin on my face. He said, "how's mom?" I told him, "heartbroken as she should be. There is no human on earth that loved you more than your mother." He hung his head in shame. "I miss them (as he paused). I would love to touch her face again. I listen to her talk to me every day. I listen for hours and cry with her. I want to tell her I am fine, and everything is ok." I said, "wait, you can hear her talk to you? Show me." He walked me to an open spot where we could see the earth. He said if you stand where you can see the earth and think about the ones you want to hear.... their voices are raised to your ear. This is how God hears your prayers every day. He listens. Mom cries a lot and prays. Dad will join in sometimes, but mom, she does not stop." I wiped a tear from my face remembering my encounter with his mother as I told her that her son had passed. "Jacob, tell me everything you know of this place, and show me how to become a warrior." He laughed and said, "shep, you already know it. It is in you. You just have to find it." I sat there staring at him like "what???" "They told me the same thing when I came up and it took me a while.... but I found it, and so will you." I really did not understand what he was saying but I took it for what it was. Jacob said, "Shep, I am going to train with the men. Come over when you can." I said, "be right there." I watched him walk away until I could not see him anymore. I lost him once, I cannot let that happen again.

I looked over at Raphael and he smiled. He said, "take a minute" and he walked away. I was alone and I thought "a minute for what?" I looked around and it was beautiful up here and as I looked around my eyes came upon the clearing where I could see the earth. I slowly walked to it and stared at earth. I concentrated on my wife and I could hear her sobbing. As I concentrated more and listened, I could see her. She was in my chair and looked like she had not been asleep in a week. She was in my NAVY sweatshirt and there were about two boxes worth of Kleenex scattered on the floor. A tear fell from my eyes. I heard her say "I miss you so much." I slowly mouthed "I miss you too." I thought of Gesa and she was in her room playing with her dolls and cars. I watched her for what seemed like days. So beautiful and how will she ever understand what happened? I love her so much. Who was going to teach her to be a warrior like her daddy was? I held my fingers to my lips and kissed them, then blew it to her. I steadied myself and cleared my eyes to start my training with my new team. I picked up my Trident and as I turned, I looked at it and noticed something. All the guys had Bright shiny Gold Tridents. Mine was too except my middle spear was red. Why? I harnessed it on my back as I came to a trot to join the team.

XIII

As I arrived at the training grounds, I saw all kinds of fighters with different styles, different weapons of all shapes and sizes. I watched for a minute amazed at how fast these defenders were. We had archers, swordsmen, spear throwers, and of course, we had the tridents. Some were with shields and some were not. I wondered why so many different styles of fighting. I watched the swordsmen as they fought in threes. One would move to cut off the head and then to stab through the heart from the front. One would move and stab from the back and the other would stab as if he were going straight down through the neck hole to get to the heart. The Archers would work in fours. Three would aim for the heart and one for the head. The spear throwers were on target. The head of their spear was abnormally large. The target they were practicing on had a fake heart on it and as they would throw the spear tip would pierce the heart, drive through it and the larger part of the back of the spearhead would cut it in half. So, by analogy, it looks as if the heart is the kill zone. As I walked along with each group, I saw the focus they had in their eyes and the determination to each and every move precise. I could appreciate that from being in the teams.

I remember when I got orders to my first team on earth. My commander was a hard ass and he believed in being able to do things in your sleep. We would go over and over the same moves hundreds of times where it seemed we were just going through the motions. Then, he would change it up and catch us off guard. We would pay for it with runs or nice long swims in the cold winter shark-infested waters off San Diego. Even long, very long, runs on their beautiful beaches.

This gave me an idea. I grabbed my trident and stood close to a target the swordsmen were practicing on. As they went into their pattern, I pushed it away. They stood there and looked at me. I just sat there and stared back at them. Finally, I said "come on, what are you going to do when your target moves." Immediately the commander of the Swordsmen flew over to me and got in my face. He looked at my feathers very snidely and said, "what are you doing?" "Observing," I said. "please tell me what you are observing," he said with the voice so snide I could hear the sarcasm. I told him that, "I was simply watching how precise his men were with a still target, but did not adapt when the target moved away from the set position." He said, "it is not your place to watch over "my" men. You have a team of your own and an exceptionally long time to train them," as he mocked my feathers. On Earth, this would have been grounds for a flat out ass woopin, but since I was new and didn't want to ruffle any "feathers" I said, "very well" and walked away as his men gathered behind him gawking at me as I was leaving.

I made it to my men and watched them fight. These were all Navy Seals on earth, and you could see the dedication in their faces. Each one had a purpose and they were going over and over the drilling as I watched. When one of the newer guys would mess up or get "fake killed," one of the senior guys would come in and show him what he did wrong, how to avoid it again and the different options he had to stay on the target, and complete the objective. I was proud of them. How would I come in and show them something different? They seem to know what is needed and they do it very well.

As I walked up to them, I yelled, "HOOOOYAH!!!!" They all stopped and cheered, "HOOYAH!!" I said, "Gentlemen, I am humbled. I watch you in your drills and you move like you know all of it. As a leader, I am asking what do I bring to the table for you? I am the one that needs YOUR leadership in teaching me how to fight in the skies. Where do I start?" There was silence and one Seal stepped forward and said, "you will start like all of us did, with each one of us." I said, "what does that mean?" Jacob stepped forward and said, "Shep, each one of us is better in one thing than the other. Whether it be a little faster, our aim is better, or what have you. You will train with each of us. We will show you how to use the Trident as it was meant to be used, to slay evil. We will show you every way "we" do things and you will develop your own skills." I looked at him and looked at the rest of the guys. There was silence for about 30 seconds as they stared at me. I said, "on one condition." They stood silent. "You bust my balls every single time until I get it right!" "WITH PLEASURE," I heard a voice in the crowd followed by laughter. I chuckled and said, "now that we have that straight ....Where do we begin." One stepped forward and said, "with me." As the others got back to training, I stayed with my first trainer. He began to go over how the Suhtan move and fly, the different levels and how we have figured out their patterns, and at what level of the devil's protection. It seems there are six levels of protection for the devil and we have figured out three.

As the day went on, I went through a few instructors. There was so much to learn. I thought I was trained and on earth and I was, but my pro down there was my novice up here. Jacob came to me as the sun started to fade and asked, "how did it go Shep?" "It's very frustrating," I told him." "I am used to being in control and leading others, and yet I have no control or so it seems and being led by all of you," He laughed and said, "it will come." "You always taught us on earth that you encouraged leadership...so do these guys, and they need someone strong that breeds calm. You are it my friend. Do you remember in buds when we took our rubber boats into the surf and we had to learn to be in sync, not only with each other, but with the sea in order to get across the waves and make it safely? We had to figure it out together as one. We all sucked at it the first few times if you remember. But as you were made to do it repeatedly, we succeeded, and we overcame and met the objective, RIGHT?" I looked at him and asked, "so is this (BUDS in the sky)?" He smiled and said, "yep" and got up and walked away. I sat for a few and I was tired both physically and mentally. I got up and dusted myself off and happened to see an open space in the sky. I slowly walked to it hoping to hear joy but knowing I would hear pain as I concentrated on my wife and daughter. I stood there and I hear my wife tell Gesa. "Gesa, why don't you write daddy a letter." I saw her put the paper on the table with a crayon and gently guided her to the table with her hand on the back of Gesa's head. She knelt and gently brushed her hair from her face. She looked at her and said, "do you want me to brush your hair as you write?" She said, "ok mommy."

"der daaaaaaddy, I mis u an mommy dos to. We playd with my dolls today. I mis u sooooo much. Wy did u leve us? Are you coming hom soon? Luv Gesa."

Tears poured from my eyes as I fell to my knees. I wept for what seemed like hours. I miss them. I miss my wife and I miss my daughter so much. I cannot even explain it to them what happened. They would never believe what really happened and what I am doing now. I must communicate with them somehow. And that is when I knew I was going to have to find a way to earth without anyone seeing me. I HAD to see them and let them know I was ok.

JUST THEN the skies lit up and the trumpets sounded. My men came running and stood in front of me. Jacob said, "They are coming." Raphael showed up and said, "They are coming for you." They know you are untrained and weak up here and it is the best chance they have to get you." They will bring everything they have to get you. I looked at him and I looked at my men. "HOOOOOOYAH," I yelled. "HOOYAH," they yelled back as they raised their tridents. Raphael COMMANDED "four with Shep… surround him!!!" I said, "GET IN THE FIGHT" as we all flew in formation of 10 seal pods. We passed the spears men, the archers, and the swordsmen. WE…. were first in the fight. We had the lead. We were faster than the rest. We flew in pods, but the pods would change shapes to look bigger, then smaller with no particular pattern. Jacob said, "this is to look like more than we are. Just like we did with firepower in the teams." I could see a dark cloud rising and the screams got louder as it got closer. We were at full speed as I yelled, "GENTLEMEN…. LEAVE NO DOUBT!!!" I then said in an exceptionally soft voice "Deliver us from evil" and then we clashed.

It was like an explosion and total chaos at first. All I heard was screaming and the Tridents bludgeoning the Suhtan. The Archers were shooting over us piercing the hearts, as the Swordsmen cut off their heads to crush their souls. I was wielding my trident the best I could and "my protectors" were doing a great job keeping them off me. I watched the fight as I fought. I watched the patterns of the Suhtan. How they moved and how basic this first band of fighters were. They were right, it was like they were trying to tire us out. With all the watching I was not paying attention and found myself outside my protection. SUDDENLY, I was grabbed by two of the Suhtan and we plummeted toward earth. Each of them had one arm and I was facing back looking at the battle take place. I was yelling for help. My trident had been knocked from my grasp. Do they not see me? I yelled again and at this point I was not going down without a fight. I kicked one of the Suhtan and broke free with one hand. I tried to break free of the other, but his grip was too tight. I yelled, "I have fought bowls of pudding that have put up more a fight than this." The one I broke free from was fighting to take control of me again and I saw a spear go straight through him and he exploded. I heard my name "SHEP…CATCH" as my trident was tossed to me. I grabbed it with my free hand and shoved it into the chest of my capture and he exploded. Both of their blood went up and suspended. Tridents and spears flew past me at crazy speeds. I turned and saw hundreds of Suhtan coming up to get me again. What seemed like a rainfall of spears and tridents were effective in killing most of them. My defenders surrounded me as we flew back to the battle. There were a few Suhtan left, but most had retreated to earth or the hole they came from. Raphael came to me and said, "are you ok?" I looked at him then my team and told him "everything went as planned." I saw my four protectors look at me like "I can't believe he just took up for us." The other Seals looked at each other and just nodded their heads. I flew up to the four protectors that were assigned to me and they had their heads down. I told them "worry not my brothers for I have failed in the field of battle as well. Let us not dwell on what happened but how we can keep it from happening again." They slowly lifted their heads as I put my hands on their shoulders and said, "now who's going to show me how we clean this evil pile of shit up," as I pointed to the suspended blood. The four in unison said, "we will."

We all flew up to the horde of blood. They showed me how we locked hands and held them high with one another in a circle, then a circle around us and a circle around that one and so on and so on. The Archers stood the watch to intercept a second attempt as we were vulnerable in this formation. I watched as the defenders would stand the perimeter of the blood gently keeping it together by waving their wings gently around all sides to keep it in one mass with no stray drops. As the blood of the Suhtan fell through our wings it was cleansed into rain so that only fresh water would fall to earth. It was heavy and felt like it was going to rip my wings off, but we held the load. I asked Jacob, "why does it feel heavier than water, but it is still a liquid?" He said, "the amount of evil is the reason. Just wait until we fight the last three levels of the devil's protection." I just stared at him. He smiled and told me "you're welcome."

We all stayed until the last drop was cleansed. When we were done the bigger circle peeled away first and took a defensive stance. Then the next one peeled away and did the same. Each circle would peel away and when the last one (the inner circle) lifted to guard, the first ring would take another position above us and then the next and then the next. Each circle would move up one by one until we were in safety where we could fly together in one formation. It was amazing how they did this

It reminded me of training on earth in the seal teams where we would lay suppressive fire on the enemy. If we needed to take another position, bug out, or get to an extraction point. We would tap the next guy on the shoulder, get to the end of the team. That guy would throw crazy rounds down range and then tap the next guy in line. This is how we communicated and got the hell out of dodge safely and effectively.

Back with the brigades we checked each other for any wounds or ripped wings. The men looked well adapted to caring for one another. I made sure I told one of the guys to get a count to make sure we all made it back. I walked through the men and patted them on the shoulder, asked them if they were ok. I made sure I thanked them and told them good job. Raphael and Gabriel hastily showed up and asked me to talk to them. I told them absolutely and I saw Jacob at about 30 yards with an intense stare. We got about 20 yards from the men and Gabriel said, "what happened out there?" I told him, "we were under attack, the men fought as I tried my best to help them." Gabriel said, "cut the shit man. YOU HAD FOUR PROTECTORS, you either left your protection or they failed to do their job." I was facing the men and I could see the four that were assigned to me in a huddle with Jacob. I was quiet. Gabriel asked, "WHICH ONE WAS IT?" I told him, "I left the protection fighting. It was my mistake." Gabriel threw his hands up and walked about 10 paces back and then back to me. "Do you KNOW how important it is for you to be here? Is there some reason you don't get it?" I stared at him and said, "my bad, it won't happen again." He then stated, "you're damn right it won't." As I watched him walk away with Raphael by his side, he seemed to be scolding Raphael not only with his voice but his hands too. They both then stopped as a blue hue came over the skies. A bright blue light was getting bigger as it got closer. I saw Gabriel and Raphael stand at attention as did all the protectors. I found myself in awe then caught myself mesmerized, shook my head, and stood at attention with the rest. A man, a GIANT man ascended from the heavens. His armor was shiny like a crystal glacier in the bluest purest water on earth. His eyes as blue as the color itself, but more like a Caribbean blue and almost see-through just as such. His sword as large as his body and he wheeled a spear strapped to his back. He stopped at Raphael and Gabriel. I saw them both nod several times. He placed his hand on Raphael's shoulder as he moved around him and headed my direction. I maintained my position of attention and watched as he came closer. His voice was like a cello in an orchestra as he said, "at ease Shepherd." I tried to be at ease, but I did not know who this was. Was this God? How do I act in front of God? Was he pissed? The man gently said, "I am the Archangel Michael. I command God's armies. You have been chosen for a reason and I'm glad you are here." I said, "thank you , sir." He immediately said, "its Michael, the only sir is God himself." I asked will I meet him too? Michael looked at my feathers and then looked at my face with a brief pause and said, "in time Shep, in time." "Walk with me," he said. I turned and walked with him. He asked me many questions. He asked me questions about my family, my mother, and my father. He asked me about my brother, my wife, and my daughter. He asked me about a million things. He then asked me "how were your parents to you?" I thought this was strange because I would think they would know, but I played the game. "My mother.

One of the greatest souls on earth. Would help you if you needed anything and would do everything in her power to please. A strong woman that held her faith close. Very decisive and heavy-handed when it came to raising us. I believe she was our strongest ally when it came to our strict raising. Tell God thank you, for sending me to someone that chose life and to be so gracious as to invite me into hers." Michael nodded and smiled. He then said, "you and your brother were close." I said, "yes, we lost each other for a while for both of us being too proud. We talked it out and became friends again. I love him. He was my idol growing up. How is he?" Michael said, "As you probably know he has had a hard time with your death. He blames himself for not spending more time with you." I interrupted and told him "make sure he knows that it's not his fault…we all lead different paths and mine was one that not many take." Michael then said, "I'll do that." "Your father, how was that relationship," he said? I stopped in my tracks and hesitated. I wanted to curse my father so badly but bit my tongue. I wanted to yell as loud as I could at him right then as if it were that he could hear me. I took a breath and said, "my father (as my head hung) was a good man, to all of his friends. He and I never saw eye to eye on anything. I always had to prove myself and my worth to him. It was my brother he lived his life through, and I never measured up to my brother's level with him. I was successful, I like you (but not on the same scale as you of course) commanded squadrons and many teams. I have a very loving wife and daughter (as I choked and teared up thinking of them). He never met my daughter, Gesa. He died from cancer and he and I stopped speaking two years prior to his death. Did he (as I hesitated) make it to heaven?" Michael said, "tell me more about your father." "We never settled anything, and I blame him for everything in my life and know I should not. I cannot forgive him......I CAN'T as I raised my voice." Michael sat and stared at me for a time. He then said, "tell me about your wife and daughter." A slow smile came over my face. My wife Rhonda, she is the most loving and forgiving human on earth. I do not......and did not deserve her. She forgave me for all my missteps in our relationship and loved me more than love itself. I always told her that she has a special place in heaven. I would give my soul to see that she goes there when it is her time. My daughter, Gesa." I could not speak for a minute. "She is every bit of bad that is in me and she has made it good if that makes sense. She is positive and strong and full of life. She is the definition of joy in this world." I fell to my knees and sobbed with my face in my hands. "I do not know how I can make it without them. They need to know I am ok." Michael slowly walked to me and put his hand on my shoulder and helped me up. "The pain you hold is great. I see your regrets; your worries, and I see your love. One day your family will have a path to heaven, but not yet. Your men like you so far. You were known to be a great leader. You were a legend on earth in the teams. We want you to continue your leadership here. Just know this.... leaders lead by example. Remember these words." We slowly walked back to the men talking about different things from expectations of me to places I need to see since I am up here that might bring a little peace to my soul. Michael stopped and looked at me and said "Shephard, you have been chosen for God's armies. I expect you will not disappoint. Great to meet you and we will see each other again soon." I said, "great to meet you too, Michael." He then turned to Raphael and Gabriel. He smiled as he talked to them and then he ascended to his post. Gabriel turned to me, nodded his head, and flew off. Raphael came to me and said, "he seemed to like you, don't mess that up." as he slapped my shoulder. "Get some rest," he said. "I will tell your men the same." I hastily said, "Raphael." He turned to look at me and I said, "I will tell them." He just smiled and nodded his head. I wiped my face and walked over to the men. As I came upon them, the leader of the swordsmen came over to me and stopped about four feet from me. He looked at me and he looked at my men as they got closer. I held my hand up to my men as to say, "it's ok." He said my name is Jerry, I was a fireman on earth. I said, "nice to meet you, Jerry." I then started to say, "hey back there when I moved your target" and he stopped me. I was going to say I'm sorry, but he said, "We saw what you did protecting your guys when you separated from your protection during the battle." I just looked at him. He then said, "it takes a true leader to do that. What can we do to help you be ready for the next one?" I gently smiled at him and grabbed his arm as a brother would in comradery and said, "just let us know what we can do for you guys to defeat the Suhtan." He said, "consider it done" smiling from ear to ear. As he walked away, I turned to my men. I looked them over as I did my team on earth. Slowly so I could see through their eyes. They stood silent anticipating my every move. I said "gentlemen ....thank you. Thank you for keeping each other safe, keeping me safe, and being the sheepdogs of the heavens." Then in a quiet almost undetectable voice I said, "Hooyah," AND THE HEAVENS ROARED LIKE THUNDER WITH HOOYAH. I laughed and said, "GET SOME REST, make ready for what comes next."

I watched them all walk away in hopes that they would get some good rest. I needed to clear my head and rest as well. So much has happened in so little time and yet is still unbelievable to me that this is not some sort of dream I am having. Did I die on earth? Do I now command an army in the skies? Most of all, how was I going to get to earth unknowingly to others to see my family?

XIV

It is funny to think that we do actually sleep up here. Even our souls need rest and healing. It is no different than when on earth that we see so much negative throughout the day that we must find a "happy place" to regenerate the goodness in us; otherwise, we just turn into very unhappy people through life. Although I do not see any unhappiness here, we are on a constant state of alert, but for the most part, I see calm in all the Defender's faces. I keep thinking what Raphael said when he was showing me around upon arrival and laying the rules down. "A month here is like a year down there." This means my daughter will be 15 within a year's time. I cannot fathom not seeing her grow up and now it will be quicker than ever. Missing all her successes and not being there when she needs me with every failure. Her proms, first dates, and her sports accomplishments. Thinking about them I stepped over to an opening in the sky. I saw my wife Rhonda watching Gesa coloring in the living room. I scanned the house to make sure the doors were locked and that she had her pistol with her. Not that I could do anything about it, but it made me feel better knowing that her head was still on right through all of this. Rhonda was trained well, and she knew how to use a weapon. I hope she teaches Gesa the same way I taught her when she gets old enough. I never want anything bad to happen without them having a fighting chance to defend themselves.

I watched Gesa coloring in what looked like a new coloring book. She had a brand-new box of crayons too. Gesa was talking a hundred miles a minute to my wife as she colored. My wife was just smiling and saying, "uh-huh" and "really" and it made me smile. Just as I was relaxed the trumpets blared again and heavens sirens went off all around us. My men came running. Both Raphael and Gabriel came over. We have a situation. A scout team of Suhtan has been spotted over New York. This usually means that they are looking for someone they want bad. Someone that will strengthen their ranks. We need to send a team to low-level surveillance to see who they are looking for. If we can identify them, we might be able to save them from the Suhtan. They will not be defenders, but we can keep evil from getting stronger by taking "their" chosen. I said, "ok…how many do you send and who is going with me?" They said, "you are not going. You are still too new. Pick a team of 10 and Raphael will go with them." I said, "TO HELL WITH THAT, I am not picking 10 of my guys and putting them in danger while I sit and watch from the cheap seats. So, I will pick 10 but I am going to be number 11." "Very well," Gabriel said, "but you stay

close to the team. DO NOT get distracted, understood."
"Aye Aye sir," I said. I called Jacob and said, "pick your guys
and let us get in the fight." It was not but minutes passed,
and we were on our way over New York City.

We came in with the clouds to disguise ourselves
as we monitored and looked for Suhtan. "There they are,
about 2 o'clock" one of my guys called out. I said, "watch
them closely men. Don't lose track of them." As they
watched the Suhtan, I pulled Jacob over and said, "now
we are going to try to figure out who they are looking for.
Scan the area and start profiling people that look like bait."
There were so many people around so finding which one
they wanted was going to be hard. There were homeless,
businesspeople, musicians, and people exercising too. Sure,
there were people that looked suspicious all around....it
was New York for God's sake. The Suhtan would hover
then move, hover then move in no particular pattern. I was
like, "c'mon creeps...show us your hand." I could not just
sit and watch. I told Jacob "don't take your eyes off me."
He said, "what are you going to do?" I told him that, "he
needed to trust me." I then shot down to earth right at the
tree line. I would move tree to tree to hide from the Suhtan.
Anything I could get behind I would move as I followed
them to see if I could watch their eyes if they stared for any
amount of time at any one target. Still nothing and in a
matter of minutes, they were gone. Not one person in this
whole city block was chosen by them. I scanned the people
again and again trying to find a clue of who they were trying to grab. Nothing came to me. I flew back up to Jacob
and gathered the men and asked, "did anyone see anything

that might have given their plan away?" All of them said, "no…we just saw them flying around." Jacob turned and faced the other way sternly whispering in my ear "you are going to get hurt…that wasn't smart." I patted him on the back and said, "I had you covering me…nothing could have happened." I barked "make note of the of where we are at, they may come back to this spot again. Let us get back to safety and debrief the Arch's." We started to ascend, and I noticed my guys were circled around me. Protecting me as we got the hell out of there. It made me smile to think they trusted me to lead them.

It reminded me of a time with my Team on earth. It was me and Sutter in an overwatch position from the roof at some bad guys that were getting ready for something. Well, that something was us and we did not know we had been seen. We started taking heavy fire from these guys and more appeared out of nowhere all around us. We were pinned down and the rest of my Team saw we were in trouble. Big Mitch had planted some C-4 on the back of the building and waited for this bunch to try to flank us. As soon as they hit the door, Mitch blew the charges and half the building went up. My guys came in, got us off the roof, and surrounded me guarding all angles of attack until we made it to the hummers. THAT is a team!!!

As we traveled up, I was looking at how beautiful the universe was. It was literally amazing how much color and how many planets were up here. It was an amazing sight. Gabriel met us at the entry and asked me what we saw. I told him that they just hovered and then flew with no pattern at all. I tried to scan the people, but no one stuck out. He said, "their target was there, it just wasn't time to pick them up. I will tell our scouts to keep watch and tell us if they see any more movement." I told Gabrielle that was a good idea and that they might have been just seeing who was weak. He nodded his head then turned and walked away. I hesitated and thought, I was back on earth and only Jacob knows I was there. Is it that easy to get there? I think I have just found my way to see my family.

The next day I went to the Arch's and told them that I have a plan. I wanted to have my own scout team so I can intercept incoming suhtan and profile what type of human or humans they are looking for. Gabriel was like "I don't think that is a good idea. You are very wanted by them and we cannot afford to have you taken." I said "c'mon, I have my team with me, and they won't let anything happen to me. I will be incredibly careful and the first sign of any danger I will sound the alarm." As I stood there watching Gabriel tossing it back and forth in his head, Raphael spoke up and said. "I think it is a good idea. From what I witnessed of him on earth he has a strong head and knows his surroundings very well." Gabriel then said, "fine, we will run a few test runs and see what you guys come up with and go from there. But the first sign of danger and you make sure you are heading north." "Aye Aye," I said to Gabriel and winked at Raphael thanking him for his two cents he threw in. Now that I had the permission, I had to pick a team that would allow me to do my thing on earth as we scouted. I now knew how I was going to see my wife and kid.

XV

A few days past and I had picked a team that I believed to be the best of the best. Jacob of course was my lead pick. We got a call that the Suhtan was in over the west coast of America and we needed to get down there and scout it out. This was awesome because my family was on the west coast too. We had moved to San Diego when I joined the military because I knew beyond a shadow of a doubt that I was going to be a NAVY SEAL and that is home base for SEAL training. We moved to the mountains of Escondido and we loved it there. Rolling hills and great views. A very peaceful place and far enough from the base if shit ever hit the fan, I knew my family would be safe.

My team and I made haste to the west coast of America. We were not ready for what we saw when we got there. There were about 500 Suhtan. We were a group of 10 on our scout team. Greatly outnumbered I told one of my guys to rush back north and send for a brigade. I feel something is going down and it was not going to be good. I told my men to stand ready from a distance. We could not take the chance on even one of those black souls getting wind of us or seeing us. We watched from a distance and they were circling Los Angeles. I asked my guys if they heard of anything going on and one of them said, "when is there NOT something going on in L.A.?" I thought "this is true," but was not prepared to see 500 suhtan. The sun was bright and almost in our face. I saw a reflection hit one of the suhtan and it stopped. I looked back and one of my guys Trident was reflecting the sun from its gold shaft. I barked "secure your trident" ....it was too late, three suhtan had broken away from the pack and were heading right to us. I told my men "easy men, I don't think they have seen us yet." As they came closer, I said "easy, eaaaaaaaaasy now." Jacob and another teammate were with me by my side and I told them if they come within 20 yards we are going to raise up and pierce their hearts with our weapons. I kept repeating who was going to throw where and they were on a path straight to us. At 20 yards I yelled "NOW." The three of us stood up and tridents were on their way. I hit mine dead in the heart as did Jacob hit his. My other teammate hit Jacob's target as well. The third suhtan that did not get hit started to SCREEEEEEAAAAAAAAAAAAAM and send the signal to their army they had brought. "MEN, ON ME," I yelled. All I saw was a black cloud coming and it was coming fast. "PERIMETER," I barked, and as each man fell in place, we had made a circle to protect all sides. I glanced north in hopes to see a brigade and there was only blue sky. As the suhtan came closer I barked "GET YOU SOME" and hell broke loose. We were hit from all sides and all we could see was darkness. I had my wings being pulled and I kicked at whatever I could. I used the front and shaft of my trident to stay alive. My guys were fighting for their lives and I hear Jaker call out "SHEP" …. he was in a fight with about 5 of his own and it was not going well. I lunged over to help him as my team closed the gap. My trident thrusts were hard and heavy on whoever tried to take Jacob. I made sure they felt each prong of my weapon. Jacob was fighting off one and one had his wings. He was at their mercy. I thrust my trident through one of the black souls that had him. We were not going to last long like this. I yelled, "COVER, COVER," telling my men to come together. This was the only way we were going to survive. The tighter we were to each other the less angle they had, and we could fight 3/1 instead of 10/1. It was an all-out battle. Everywhere I turned I did not even have to look if one was there because they were. I was thrusting and kicking at every black creature that came along. Our shields were dented and torn. We were doing everything we could, and it was not looking good. Just then I heard the trumpets sound and 1000 spears flew past us and into the dark cloud. Swordsmen clashed with the suhtan as if they were a missile locked on a target. The sound was deafening. The battle was now in our favor and we had surrounded the Suhtan. We had them at every angle and my men seemed to have gotten their second wind and they were not about to let any of them escape. The blood of the evil was suspending above us and it was a big pool this time. Evil one after evil one was losing the battle to the Brigade and as we fought until there was no evil left, we realized that we had killed them all. Some of my guys fell to their knees in exhaustion. I was panting like a fat dog that had just gone on a 10-mile hike. I surveyed the area as I saw the last swordsmen thrusting their weapons into the hearts to make sure none survived. As the brigade came over to me, I hugged Jaker and asked him if he was ok. He smiled that smile with those long black locks and said, "you saved my ass" and I said "no sir, the brigade saved OUR asses. "Gentlemen, you are true warriors and thank you for getting here when you did. I did not see this going well for us if you would not have come," saying this as I was out of breath and beat up. I looked at the hoard of blood above us and looked at the brigade and said, "shall we?" We began to get into position to cleanse the blood of the evil. We were the storm that earth just witnessed and now we are going to make it rain. "Let not one drop fall to earth so that this evil not prevail" I barked.

While in the cleanse there was so much evil, and it was heavy. We would be here a while and the archers were watching for any sign of the Suhtan, as they protected us during this process. I heard guys joking and laughing out loud during the cleanse like old drunken sailors that had just won a mockup War Game that the Navy used to keep our battle groups ready. I told Jaker that I was worried when he called out as if it were my son calling for his father. He smiled and said Shep, "I owe you." I told him, "that he had paid any due with me he had with his voucher. That I would never know how to fully repay him for this selfless act." He just said "my pleasure" and I said, "you have had too many trips to Chick-fi-A" Jaker. He smiled and said, "Is there such a thing as too many trips to Chick Fil A? We are talking God's Chicken now." We both laughed hard and as my head tilted to the sky in laughter, I saw a drop of the Suhtans' evil blood that had gone errant. It was in my reach or so I thought. I reached out with my hand to grab it, but the weight of the evil going through my wings shortened my reach and it went right through my fingers. I yelled, "ONE DROP, ONE DROP GOT AWAY.... IT'S HEADING TO EARTH." I heard them yell, "STAY IN THE CLEANSE." I told them I can get it, and they quickly told me "DON'T MOVE OR WE LOSE IT ALL." "Jacob, watch that drop with me. Do not let it out of your site." I was frantic. I kept looking at the hoard and then the drop. Back and forth as the hoard got smaller so did the drop. I was chomping at the bit to break away and dive to earth to keep it from hitting. The trumpets sounded and the cleanse was through. I immediately dove to earth. I was flying as fast as I could to get this drop. I was not going to let evil fall to earth on my watch. I heard Jacob yell, "NO!!!!" It was too late I was on my way and in a hurry. I knew I could grab it. As I got closer to it, it got closer to earth. I saw a crowd of people and it was raining fresh cleanse. It was hard to keep track of the evil drop, but I had it in my sight. I was almost to it. It landed on a kid's nose so I would not be able to grab it. I would have to wing it off. As I reared back to blow it off his nose it was too late. The drop ran down his nose and into his mouth with rain running down his face. I SLAMMED to the ground with such force the earth shook. I stared at the kid and thought about what can I do, but "nothing" was the only thing that came to my head. I fell to my knees looking up in the rain. "WHYYYYYYYYYYYYYYY," I screamed. Why did you let an innocent kid get infected with the blood? I watched the kid as he walked away unknowingly changed his life. My team met me what seemed like minutes after I touched earth. I must follow him and see where he lives…I HAVE TO DO SOMETHING. Jacob said, "there is nothing you can do Shep. We must go…it is not safe here." I took off and followed the boy to his house and my team followed. I went in with him as he walked into his room and dispersed of his wet clothing. I looked around the room. His name was Blaine and he was just a normal kid. I saw his sports pictures and a family picture he had on his nightstand. I saw trophies and a coin collection he was making on his wall. He could not be more than 8. My daughter's age at this point. His parents do not have a clue and now they do not have their kid anymore. My heart sunk. I came out of his house slowly with my head hung low. "Come," Jacob said. "We must leave now." I said, "how can this happen to good people?" My team lifted me up almost throwing me into the air. I watched his home get smaller as we went north. I felt guilty. It will be my duty to watch over this kid now. I cannot even imagine what is going to happen to him. What is going to happen to his family? I cannot allow him to be turned into evil and not live a normal life. I must ask if this has ever happened when I see the Archs. I must know if it has and how it turns out. As a father of my own, I am in shambles now knowing Blaine's life would never be the same.

We returned to the heavens and were met by Gabriel. He did NOT look happy. "Report," he barked. I told him, "We were well disguised in our location and we maintained distance. It was not due to negligence, the sun reflected from one of our weapons for a split second, but it was long enough to draw attention. We had a miscommunication on the acquired target. It will not happen again." Gabriele barked at me and questioned whether I was fit to lead this team. I sat quietly and listened as he ranted on and on. He then said, "I have the inclination to take you off the scout team." I told him, "I would ask you to reconsider." He then said, "you've shown incompetence and need more training." I then said, "I strongly advise you not to do this" as my voice got stronger. He said "NO"…this is best that you return to the heavens for more training. It was then that I barked back at him. "I WILL NOT COMPLY." He looked at me in astonishment. I started to walk to him. "YOU HAVE SHOWN DISCONTENT FOR ME SINCE I GOT HERE. WHETHER IT BE MY POSITION OR THAT ONE OF MY MEN VOUCHED FOR ME TO GET HERE INSTEAD OF DOWN THERE. YOU HAVE QUESTIONED MY EVERY MOVE AND ABILITY IN LEADING THIS TEAM. I GET IT, I HAVE MORE COLOR IN MY WINGS THAN ANYONE; BUT THAT IS NO EXCUSE TO TREAT ME LIKE "IM NOT WORTHY." WE ARE ALL WORTHY HERE AND I AM MORE THAN CAPABLE OF LEADING THIS TEAM. Do I need guidance (as my voice went to calm), yes. Will I need more training? yes, we all must constantly train to maintain our edge. BUT WILL I ALLOW YOU TO CHASTISE ME ALONE MUCH LESS IN FRONT OF MY MEN WITHOUT SAYING SOMETHING.................. NO." I began to see my men gather behind me. "I WILL TAKE ALL THE BLAME FOR MYSELF AND MY MEN. IF SOMETHING GOES AREYE I ALONE WILL TAKE THE BLAME. But to take someone away from something that is good only to satisfy your fears is not acceptable. We had a glitch, but we know how to fix it now. This is what we do. We adapt and we overcome. Could things have turned out bad.......... YES. Did they.......... NO. THANKFULLY, the brigade showed up and engaged or it would have been bad. REALLY BAD!!!" (Unannounced to me the whole brigade was now standing behind me.) I continued to speak. "THE SUHTAN TOOK MY LIFE AWAY FROM ME. THEY......... TOOK MY FAMILY. I WAS THE TARGET. Is there anyone else among us that they have wanted so badly?" It was silent. I asked again "well....is there?" Gabriele calmly said "no." I continued "THEY ATTACKED ME AND NOW ITS PERSONAL FOR ME. They took everything I know that was good away from me. My wife and kid do not know where I am or what happened. MY TEAM questions my very sanity as to what really happened. The Navy is saying it was a chute malfunction. THEY DON'T KNOW." I hesitated and looked around. Gabriel's eyes never left me. I turned to my men and to the brigade that was backing me up. "THESE MEN!!! THEEEEEESE MEN FIGHT FOR YOU AS DO I. WE DEFEND HEAVEN HERE IN THE SKIES

AS WE DEFENDED "OUR HEAVEN" THERE ON EARTH. Each one of us has a stake in this. Each of us wants evil vanquished so badly so that others, on earth, can live in peace." As I turned back to face Gabriele again and said, "let me do what I know how to do. Let me train and be trained. If you will grant me this, then we cannot fail." Jacob came to my side and stood in solidarity with me as we all looked at Gabriel. He scanned the brigade and looked at me with a smile and said, "you said something right, one of your feathers, is now white." With that, he ascended to his post. I slowly turned to the brigade and said, "WHO'S IN THE FIGHT?" and the earth heard loud thunder as the men screamed, "HOOYAH!!"

XVI

The next day at the training grounds I was in the mirror looking at my lone white feather. Man, this looked good. The guys were rousing me asking where I got my new digs. Jacob was laughing at me and telling me that "it's going to fall out." I told him from his lips to God's ears. I do not know what part of it that I said made this happen, but it was nice seeing that I too could have feathers like the rest. I saw Gabriel and Raphael coming my way. I met them halfway and immediately told Gabriel "I'm sorry for the way I spoke to you. It was not of anger toward him, but passion for how I believed I am perceived here. I told him that I will accept any punishment he hands out." He stopped me and said "Shep, it was your "passion" that put that white feather on your back. It was your "passion" that made me rethink how we do things here. Your words rang true to all your men as I watched you talk, I watched them gather in unity behind you. NOT JUST YOUR TEAM, BUT THE WHOLE BRIGADE!!! This shows me that you ARE the leader they need. You were chosen for a reason and I will never question you again. We will learn this together because we cannot defeat evil alone." I smiled and said, "thank you" and shook his hand as if we were brothers.

We went over the situation that I saw in LA. I told him that something is taking place there and I believe it to be the epicenter of what comes next. Raphael asked, "do you have any clue why the west coast?" I said, "no, there are many places on earth that hold more evil that would be better suited for a base." Look at Chicago. You have a melting pot of races and religions. ALL these people are good at heart, but have been made to believe that they must be bad to be accepted. I bet if you ask any one of the people there if they are at peace, they would say no. I bet not one of them would tell you that this is what they dreamed of doing as a child. Look at all the places on earth that evil has taken over. Where people kill people for anything and everything, I bet there is an absence of love, family, and most of all God. To take another's life just to prove worthiness to someone else should throw a red flag." Jacob said, "in the absence of family these kids cling to anything that they can call family and bond to that with their loyalty. It is hard to break that once they do this." I agreed with Jacob. He is correct in that statement. All I know is we need to concentrate and listen to the chatter in LA. If there is enough evil there, we will hear it from the people. Gabriel said "tell me what the game plan is and let us go over it. I will wait for your report."

As Gabriel left, I sat back and thought of my wife and Gesa. I walked over to an opening and thought of them.

My wife was working, and my daughter was in school. I scanned the house and discovered a letter Gesa had written to me.

Dear Dad,

I miss you. I hope you do not mind me writing to you all the time, but it is my way of staying close to you and making sure you know I have not forgotten you. I do not even know if you can see me or mom much less see what I am writing, but it gives me peace to believe you can. I hope wherever you are that you are smiling. I miss your smile. Although I was young, I remember everything about you. Your smile made me smile and your strength made me strong. It was my 15th birthday two days ago. I hope you are looking down and proud of me. I have been getting A's in school with one B in math. I hate math. I like a boy but do not think he likes me. We have classes together and we talk. I hope he asks me to Junior prom, but I will not get my hopes up. Mom is doing better. The years have been kind to her, and she is strong. She refuses to date anyone. She says her heart was given long ago, and she has nothing left to give anyone. I do not want her to be lonely, but I love that her love for you was so absolute. I hope I find that love one day.

I will write again soon and know I love you. I miss you dad, very much.

~Gesa

My heart aches. I miss her so much and I miss my wife. I thought of Blaine and wanted to check in on him. His room was different and when I looked at the house they had moved. He was listening to music in his room with his headphones laying on his bed. His letterman's jacket hanging over the chair at his desk. He has lettered in baseball and football. I thought maybe the blood drop did not affect him, he seems like he has his head on straight. I looked over his room and then back at the jacket. I got a little closer when something caught my eye. His jacket was from the Escondido Padres. Escondido High! That was the same school as Gesa!!!!!! I looked back at him and he suddenly stood straight up in his bed and was looking around as if he was trying to find something, or was it that he was trying to find.....................me?

XVII

Jacob came to me with a plan that he felt would keep us safer while we were scouting at a low level. I agreed to the plan and told him we would present it to the Arches. We approached them with a plan. We would send a low-level team to scout, but there would be a team within sight watching us. There would then be a team within sight of that team and so on all the way up. This would ensure the message "IF ATTACKED," would get to the brigade faster and would allow each team to join the fight once they sounded the alarm up to the next. They championed this plan and said, "great job Shep." I quickly told them that I had nothing to do with this. That it was all Jacob. He alone figured this out. Gabriel turned Jacob and said, "it is no surprise to me." He then told Jacob great job. I could see the proudness in Jacob's face as he stood straight up and smiled. It was awesome to see the gratitude toward him. I quickly told the Arches that we were going to brief the men and get ready for a low level in LA. Raphael said, "keep us in the loop." We both returned "Aye Aye" as sailors do.

The men mustered and we went over the plan on how we would descend, and I had Jacob pick nine captains that would stage their teams and he told them all at what levels they would stage. It was awesome seeing this kid lead. He was born for this. His mother would be so proud.

XVIII

The next day we mustered up and went over the mission. Who would do what, where we would be if this or that happened, and the target in which we were looking for. As we descended to our stages the teams of ten would break off at their given altitude. Once it was the scout team left, we slowed our approach to make sure to come in quiet and unnoticed. We scanned the area for Suhtan, but there was no activity. We looked and looked, but we did not see even one Suhtan. I grabbed Jacob and told the team that we were going lower and to keep watch. Jacob and I went down and walked among the humans. Everything was normal. We saw some irritated conversations on the cell phones, but no evil was felt, or should I say nothing deadly. We ascended back to the team and briefed them on what we saw. We signaled the first stage that we were coming back up and they signaled the others and so on.

The Archs met us back in the heavens and we relayed what we "didn't see." We were perplexed to say the least. I told them that something was up, and this was not normal. The first 3 levels of the devil's protection were not that clever. I went over every inch of ground we looked at to see if I could jog my memory of something I might have seen, and nothing came to mind. My team stated that they did not see any abnormal movement or even a glimpse of danger. I sat in wonder, but I know this, when my gut tells me somethings up, we better keep guard.

The next day we were going over our plan for our next mission I told the guys that we were hitting LA first and work our way down to see if we can spot something. I was doing this out of my own want to check in on my family, but the guys did not need to know this. As we descended in the stages to guard at altitude my team hovered over LA and again nothing was brewing. This was not like the Suhtan to be in one area and then totally abandon it. We started making our way south and as we got into the San Diego area, I felt a chill. Something was not right. We were coming up on Escondido and I told Jacob I wanted to stop by my house. He said, "you know that is not a good idea. We are not supposed to go to earth remember it is dangerous." I told him, "I know but I must see my wife." He said, "we must be extra careful not to get caught." I agreed and told the team to guard while Jacob and I went down to the ground.

I stopped in front of my house and hesitated. As I walked through the door without it being open, I saw my wife. She looked amazing. She was vacuuming as she always did, and our home was always clean. Our pictures were still up, and I could smell it as if it were yesterday. I sat and watched her in awe. I miss her. She was vacuuming in front of the fireplace and stopped for a minute and looked at a picture of us together that was on the mantle. I saw her put her hand over her mouth and choke back tears. She quickly looked away and continued to vacuum. I slowly walked to our bedroom. I needed her to know I was ok, but how could I give her a signal. We were not allowed to touch anything. I stood by our bed and laid my trident down on it as I squatted to look at another picture of us with Gesa the first day we brought her home. We were so proud to finally have a child. A tear came to my eye as it ran down my cheek. I do not think I will ever get over this pain. I picked my trident up and headed toward Gesa's room. Rhonda was coming through the door and past right through me. I gasped. I could smell her perfume "phantom of the opera" was her favorite. I slowly made my way to Gesa's room. She was so grown up now. Her favorite band posters on her wall and pictures of her and her friends on her nightstands and…………..I looked closely at a picture and knowing we weren't supposed to touch anything I picked it up to get a better look. It was Gesa…………with Blaine!!!! How can this happen? I looked closer and I saw an image behind them. IT WAS THE SUHTAN!!!!!! Just then I heard Rhonda Cry out "SHEP!!!!!" I RAN INTO THE ROOM. Her hands over her mouth and tears streaming down her face. She was staring at the bed. My trident had left an impression of the fork on her pillow. She fell to her knees and sobbed. I looked back in Gesa's room and yelled to Jacob, "THEY ARE AT THE HIGH SCHOOL!!!!!"

I ran out of the house and took flight to the team. "FOLLOW ME," I barked. "The Suhtan are at the high school." Jacob told me, "slow down Shep. If they are there, we do not want to sound the alarm we are coming." He was right. I needed to calm myself. We had always been taught "don't run to your death." We flew in higher than normal and I was right. As we approached the high school there was a black cloud over it. Thousands of Suhtan were guarding it as if someone they wanted was in it. I felt a lump in my throat because I knew who it was, and my Gesa was in danger.

I looked for a way in as to not be noticed, but there was no way. They had the school guarded like it was their lair. I told Jacob to send the signal we were coming up and he did. I got back to the brigades and gave my pass down to the Archs. They asked me why I was that close and what was I doing in my house. I had to tell them something, so I told them I had a hunch after seeing Blaine's lettermen's jacket with the school name on it. This was this kid that had the blood of the evil in him and now he and my daughter were obviously more than friends at this point. I found an opening to see if I could see anything and concentrated on Blaine. I found them in the halls of the high school. He was laughing with his friends standing against the lockers and Gesa was wearing his jacket. The Archs were watching with me. I saw him stop suddenly and look up and around like something spooked him or he got wind. Raphael said, "uh oh he has the evil in an advanced stage. He senses we are watching." I told him there is no way he can do that and just then he grabbed Gesa and kissed her. When he broke the kiss, he looked up as if to say, "I know who she is." My heart sunk and my anger grew. How could he have known of her and when did he find out. If he knew of her then they knew of my wife as well. "I have to do something," I yelled at the Archs. Jacob put his hand on my shoulder and calmly said, "let's make a plan"

XIX

The next day I found an opening and thought of the picture I saw. I wanted the Archs to see what I saw in it but then I saw this,

Dear Dad,

I miss you. Were you here today? Mom says that there was an impression on her pillow, and it looked like your trident. I wish it were true, but I feel she just misses you so much that if she burns toast, she will say it is a picture of you. It is not a bad thing, but I hate that she has so much pain. On a good note, that guy I was telling you about. We are dating now. He is the star quarterback for our football team and a great outfielder in baseball. He might get a scholarship but seeing is how we are only juniors he has time. Aaaaaaaaaaaaaaaand he asked me to junior prom. I am wearing a gold dress to match your trident. Mom likes him, but you know how she is always being worried about me. I will be careful.

I love you and miss you. I wish you were here to meet him. You would probably scare him though.

~Gesa

NO NO NO NO NOOOOOOOOOOOO.... how could this happen? How did I let that one drop fall through my fingers and infect this child? My sorrow for him has now turned to anger. It was no choice of his to be infected by evil, but it happened. I must stop this, and I must get them apart somehow.

My anger grew over the next few days as I was trying to come up with a way to get them apart. If Blaine were in an advanced stage, he would be able to know I was up to something. What was I going to do? I told Gesa that I would never let evil get to her and now it has. I must stay calm and figure this out. I must find a way to him.

Jacob came to me and told me "you need to sleep. You cannot stay up like this. You have to rest physically as well as your soul." "Jacob, I am beside myself. With all my training and planning of missions, I cannot seem to grasp this one. I cannot find a way to him and even if I do, what can I do to get them apart?" Jacob said, "rest, I'll keep a watch." With that, I knew he was right. I had to rest and keep my head. Maybe with that, I will be able to focus on the plan.

The next morning, I asked Jacob if there were any changes. He said, "Shep, I have watched all night and not a thing." I thanked him for being this dedicated and he told me that the guys were ready to step in when I got tired. We need to make another low level over the high school and just watch while hidden in the clouds. I need to watch the patterns and their movement to and from. Do they all stay or do they cycle in and out with other Suhtan. I need to see it and only then can I attempt to come up with a plan.

Just then the trumpets sounded, and the Heavens lit up. "REPORT," I barked, and Jacob and Jerry the Swordsman Commander came over to me. We have intercepted a movement north. A black cloud Is heading this way. I looked over to the guys and barked "MAKE READY." I turned to Jerry and said, "we have the lead" and he said, "We got your six." My guys followed me as we descended to earth and the brigade followed.

As we came down, we saw the cloud, but it was coming to us at an abnormally slow pace. I barked "at 1 o'clock" to make sure my men had their eyes fixed on them. I told Team five to scan the area so we would not be flanked. I saw them slow up in their dive to keep vantage. "Men on my go/no go." I heard a, "roger that." We were coming in hot, but as we got closer the Suhtan that were coming up started back down. They would see us and then turn to go back down. This was not like them at all. I called out "slow up" I raised my hand to hold position and I could hear the command cycle up to the heavens for the rest of the brigade. The Suhtan were hovering as if to entice us to them. I looked at them and then looked through them to earth. They were over the high school. "Somethings up," I told Jacob. "hold your position." Raphael and Gabriel both came to us. I turned to them and said, "somethings not right, they are not attacking us." We watched for a minute as they flew around in circles. I turned to Gabriel and asked "have the Suhtan every attacked us in the cleanse? He said, "a few times." I asked him "what was the outcome?" He told me that some of the cleanse got away each time and fell to earth. "What years were they?" I asked. He said, "in the late 1700s, the mid-1800s, early 1900s, almost mid-1900s and the last time early 1990s." I immediately yelled, "STAND DOWN, STAND DOWN" to the brigade and I heard the order repeated up to the heavens so that everyone was on the same page.

Gabriel asked me what I thought they were doing, and I told him this. "They are trying to infect as many kids as possible. They know that a battle will create a cleanse and they will attack with full force at that time over the high school. This will infect the young and they can groom them as they grow older." Jacob said, "kind of like on earth with the media things telling kids that good things were bad and bad things were good." I said, "EXACTLY......controlling the kids and infecting them with the evil from the cleanse assures they have allies for years to come." "They are getting smarter," said Raphael. I nodded my head and said, "yes. I believe they will pick prominent figures to infect, and those figures will help spread evil around the world and they will have to do less work." We can't fight over the school." Gabriel agreed and sounded the horn to get back to the Heavens.

As we got back to our posts, I paced back and forth racking my brain on how they are getting smarter. The only way they could do this was the devil's knowledge. He had to have people in place already. There had to be prominent people around earth that he had infected himself or were groomed to spread evil to anyone and everyone they could. These prominent figures would be like "commanders" for the Suhtan placed all over the earth but in the flesh. How do we know who they are and how do we find them? Time moves so quickly on earth, so we had to think fast, and we had to make a plan.

I asked Raphael and Gabriel for a sit down with Michael. They agreed that we needed to let him know what was going on. Maybe with all of us together we could figure this out. I grabbed Jacob and Jerry and took them to the meeting. Michael's post was amazing. You would have thought it was heaven itself. If this is not heaven, then I do not know if I can handle anything more beautiful than this. The skies up here were AMAZING, to say the least. Colors of the bluest blues and the greenest greens. I was in awe. I saw Jacob and Jerry just looking around in amazement. Michaels said, "come sit down. We have a problem I see," Michael said. As we sat down, I asked Michael "do you keep any records of earth around?" I had noticed many documents, and many books, but did not know what they were all about. He stood up from his chair and looked around the room and went to one book. "This is Earth," he said. It was a very thick book. I said what are the rest of these books if I may ask? He said this is every planet and every star in the heavens. This is every movement of anything in the universe. If you look around this is the history of all that is known and unknown to humans. This is the mystery of space. I saw one book alone and by itself on the podium. I was fixated on it. Michael saw me looking and he said, "THAT is the Holy Bible. Some on earth say it is just words while others say it is THE word. Some say it is all fake, while others believe it is the lifeblood story of humans and how we should be on earth." I looked at Michael and said, "you talk as if you don't know what it is." Michael looked at me and said, "I.........know exactly what it is, and I know its truth. "For God so loved the world, that he gave his only begotten Son, that whosoever believeth in him should not perish, but have everlasting life." You see Shep, humans get to choose what they believe and do not believe. God gave man his own free will to live in the flesh and make decisions as he saw fit. Hence your feathers," he said as he gave me a shit-eating grin. "You chose MANY bad decisions in the flesh, but we knew in your heart you were a good human. We knew you cared for others. Anytime you want to borrow it.... let me know," he said as he looked at me from the corner of his eye.

"Open the book of earth and see if it has what you are looking for," Michael said. I opened the book and was in amazement. This had to be classified material because it was a ton of information. I looked at each of the date periods Gabriel told me about. The 1700s, 1800s, and 1900s......I confirmed my belief. I said "Gentlemen, each of these periods there were great wars on earth. Evil trying to take over each time." I looked up from the book and slowly looked at the men around the table. "Evil is a progression," I said. "They attack the cleanse knowing that evil will fall to earth. They do it to put into play their "next" phase. It is a chess match gentlemen, and we have been playing checkers this whole time." "Michael," I said. "What happens when evil rules the earth?" He stood and slowly walked from the table. He came to a stop and looked out into the vast array of planets.................... "it dies," he said. "And as one planet dies another will soon be infected. Then another and another. As they all die, we cannot find defenders anymore with so much evil in them. When enough planets die as they succumb to evil, their advance on Heaven is imminent."

I looked at Jacob and then at Jerry "We have to make a run on the devil now. We have got to take out the source while we still control the heavens. We cannot wait." Gabriel and Raphael both looked at Michael who still had his back toward us. With a deep breath he slowly turned and said, "And so it begins." I smiled knowing that permission was now granted.

XX

We had to plan and plan quickly. This was the biggest mission that the heavens had ever seen, and we needed to do it right. We had one chance to surprise attack. If we failed, we would never have that element in our favor again. It was time to call a meeting with all the brigade commanders and set a plan in motion.

In all the chaos I took a minute to find a space in the sky to check on my family. I saw my wife reading on the chair in the living room. She seemed peaceful. I could sit and watch her for days. Even though time has been good, I could see the age in her face as the years have passed. She is still the most beautiful woman on earth to me. Oh, how I miss her and wish that I could hold her again. I looked for my daughter and she was in her room getting ready for school. I saw a letter on her desk, and it read...

Dear Dad,

It is our Senior year and it has been a wild ride. I graduate in less than 3 months. I imagine you at my graduation all the time. I wish I could share this with you like I should have been able too. I know you have missed so much of my life and I hope you are proud of me. Mom says I take after you a lot with my drive and purpose in life. I will be going to SDSU after I graduate. Blaine has accepted a scholarship in football there to be their "next-generation" quarterback as he always says. I love him and he is good to me. I hope you would approve of him. Mom still believes that you came to the house that day and says that she knows you are ok. Dad, I wish you were here. With you having such limited time in my life it amazes me how close I feel to you. Please stay safe wherever you are, and I hope that you are watching over me. I requested that you be my guardian Angel if that is even a thing lol. I love you and I will write again soon.

~Gesa

It tears my heart out each time I read her letters. What could have been if I were alive and could I have "scared" Blaine away from her or would he have ever been infected. Would another more experienced protector been able to catch that drop, or would there have even been a drop that escaped the cleanse? So many questions that I will never know the answer to.

I was sitting just staring into the universe when Jacob came and sat next to me and said, "you good?" I laughed and said, "yea I'm good Jacob." "Tables turned huh," I said. He laughed and said, "what are you thinking about." I sat for a minute and said, "I am thinking about all that I have missed with my family. I miss them. I miss the guys on our team. I am trying to think about how we are going to make a run at that Devil without them knowing. How can we lure him out? What is it going to take?" Jacob sat for a minute then he said, "Your family is safe for now. Although we have a problem with Blaine, your family is safe. Our team is retired now and doing their own thing. Time goes quickly up here. As for the luring the devil out...I am at a loss." I asked Jacob, "do you know if we have ever made a run at him, or do we just defend against any attacks?" He said, "I do not know. That might be a great question for the Archs. Let us set a meeting with the Brigade commanders and the Archs and hash this out."

The day had passed, and we had a meeting with the brigade commanders in the courtyard. I was speaking with Raphael and asked him if we had ever made a run at the devil. He looked around to find Gabriel and Michael and motioned them over. He said, "Shep wants to know if we have ever made a run at the devil?" Michael dropped his head and with a slight hesitation quietly said "Yes. We tried once and were heavily defeated. We thought we had him where we wanted him, and we went into his world. As we entered it looked like the Suhtan were sleeping and the brigades quietly slipped through the channel that led to him. The Suhtan were clung to the walls of his cave unknowingly awake and letting us pass. We came upon the devils three layers of protection and they were almost standing still, and we could see him sitting on his thrown with his back to us." Michael hesitated, "I then gave the order to attack and that is when I realized we were surrounded. The Suhtan had closed the corridor that we came in on. The devil's layers spun up and formed a barrier around him. He never turned around and just laughed as loud as he could as they attacked us from all sides. His head would rise to the sky as he laughed, and his arms would spread to his sides as if we were waiting to gather us into hell. We fought for our lives and somehow only lost half of what we had. Some of the Suhtan that we see today are prior defenders that he tortures endlessly." I sat there listening to this in horror. The souls of our Defenders are now tortured souls of the Suhtan. I could not believe my ears. My head dropped and Michael said, "If you can stomach it, I will show you." I looked up and he waved his hand in the air from left to right as if he were opening a curtain and there it was. The battle. In midair, it was playing out like real-time. My heart sunk as I watched our Defenders screaming for their lives. Then I was angered as I saw the devil laughing with his back to the whole thing. His three levels of protection forming a shield around him. They flew in what looked like controlled chaos with no discernible pattern it seemed. I asked, "how did you get out?" I heard Gabriel say, "We knew the first three layers of the Suhtans patterns well and I gave the order to turn and fight our way out. Little by little we were able to make ground. Knowing the Devil's shield would not leave him we had to distance ourselves so that what we were fighting was in front of us and not all around us. It worked. The Blood of the Suhtan in this battle soaked into the earth. We were not able to cleanse it nor would we have been able to with such a loss of protectors and we almost did not have enough energy to ascend back to the heavens. We sustained many, many attacks on heaven for years after. They knew we were weak, and they tried their best to get to the gates. Luckily, they were denied. It has taken us many decades to get back up to the numbers we have now. This is one reason we train so much. We vowed to never let that happen again." Gabriel then said, "you could hear his laugh all the way up to the heavens that day." I sat for a minute and asked, "Then why permission to try again, why now?" Michael stood with his back to me, turned and looked dead at me. His stare was cold, yet warm in a way if that can even happen. He slowly started to walk to me. He said "Shep, you are needed. We chose you not for your abilities on earth and God knows not for your lack of sin, but your Ethos, your heart. We saw what was in you and you truly do believe in protecting those that cannot protect themselves. You genuinely love human beings. We needed YOU. There has never been a moral compass with a truer north than yours and we needed you as a Defender. Your purpose in life unbeknownst to you was to one day help us defeat evil. Your time was cut short on earth and you came to us a little quicker than you should have, but the Devil wanted you badly. He knew that a mortal with your strength and purpose would one day be a challenge to him if you were not by his side, but by ours. THIS is why I have granted permission. We must come up with a plan and I must approve of it. We cannot have a loss as we did before if any at all." I asked him "the Defenders that are now tortured Suhtan………. can we get them back?" Michael smiled and said "yes. When they drink the cleanse once it has run through our wings before it hits earth. If they drink it in its purest form, we can turn the defenders back. We cannot save the Suhtan that left earth and went directly to hell. They are unsavable because while on earth they made the choices to do bad things after being warned time and time again." Michael said, "Shepard.............What is the plan?"

XXI

We gathered and each brigade commander brought his top 10 guys to sit in. They really did not know what we were meeting about since it was just Jacob, Jerry, and the Archs that know about this. As everyone gathered, I welcomed them in and thanked them for coming on such short notice. As I stood in front of them, I was trying to come up with a simple way of telling them the mission and concluded there is no simple way. So, I said in a noticeably confident voice "We are going after the devil." You could have heard a pin drop as they stared at me. One voice said, "do you not know what happened to us the last time?" I calmly said, "yes, I have been briefed on the battle and the outcome." Another stood up and said, "why now?" I told them, "that was a great question. Evil is growing at a rapid pace. We have our numbers back up and the Suhtan are actively searching for new recruits. Blood that has escaped the cleanse has infected many and those infected with the evil accelerate into an advanced stage of evil. They are spreaders and their powers grow more rapidly than others." One Brigade commander stood up and barked "this is about your daughter dating that kid that got infected. You are going to put all of us in danger out of selfishness to satisfy your needs." I stood in silence and stared at him. I scanned all the commanders slowly then quietly in a humble tone said, "it is true that my daughter is dating a boy that was infected by the evil. The very drop that I failed to grab was the drop that infected this child. For years it has ripped my very heart out that I am to blame for his life to change. It has tortured my soul daily to think that "only if." I have not forgotten NOR HAVE I FORGIVEN MYSELF for this." My voice started to raise now as I was getting angry. "BUT FOR YOU TO SUGGEST THAT I BE SELFISH AND PUT MY FELLOW DEFENDERS INTO BATTLE FOR "MY WANTS" IS TREADING ON TREASON. SHAME ON YOU!!!! I have not the power to take you into battle without permission nor do I have the inclination of putting anyone in danger at any given time. But (as my voice calmed) ....I do however have the knowledge of how many we are as to how many they are and right now we have the advantage and by great numbers. Evil is spreading commanders. If we do not do something now to end it or IN THE VERY LEAST...............slow its crawl. We may never get this chance again. I ask you to look at the data. Look at our trained defenders with pride. And above all that............. I ask you to trust me that I would never do anything to purposely expose you to danger or selfishly ask you to fight my battles for me. I will be the first in and last to leave. I promise you that." I saw some chatter amongst the commanders and their top ten. One commander then stood up and said "MEN, ON ME." All the brigade commanders and their men stood up and huddled in the back of the courtyard. Jacob came to me and put his hand on my shoulder. He smiled that Jacob smile and looked at me and said, "your voice scared the crap out of that guy" as he laughed a stifled laugh. "I thought he was going to cry." I held back a laugh in case anyone was watching. I looked over my shoulder to see Raphael, Gabriel, and Michael quietly watching. What were they saying? I could not hear anything, and it looked like they were all talking at once. Was I about to be kicked out of the heavens by vote? Could that even happen if I had the Archs permission to form this mission? I might have been up here for a while, but I was still the "new guy" and although I thought I had earned trust, I was about to find out how much.

The group stopped talking and the commanders stood in front of all their men. The one commander that questioned me stepped forward. "Shep, our loyalty and trust are to the Archs. It is they and God himself that we defend and protect. We have watched you with your men and they love you. We have watched you with some of the Brigade Commanders and they love you. We see a peace in the Archs faces which shows they approve of you. Lastly, you have a man that vouched HIS OWN SOUL taking a chance on you. As commanders of our brigades seeing all of this……. we trust you. We will fight with you." A smile came over my face like no other. Jacob punched me in the arm like "you did it, you bastard." The commander spoke again and said, "YOU have to tell heaven's defenders and they must trust you too. We will help." I said, "let's go talk to the men."

With that, I knew if I had the commanders on my side, we should be able to get the men to agree with no problem. We called the heavens into a tight formation. There were Defenders as far as the eye could see and beyond. There were no "loudspeakers" up here like you would speak to a crowd on earth, but you could speak normally, and all the Defenders could hear you. It was like voices carry. Even in the deepest corner of the formation, nobody was out of hearing distance. It must have been a heavenly thing. With the commanders behind me and the Archs behind them, there was a look on the men's faces of confusion of what they were about to hear. I said, "Men, Evil is upon us and growing at a rapid pace. I know you see the repetition of attacks getting more and more over the years. We are learning their patterns as they are learning ours. Evil is taking the earth right from us and if we do not stop it…… it will devour every bit of good we have ever known." They were staring at me and some were looking at each other like "where is he going with this." "I have spoken with your Brigade Commanders and we are all in agreement that we must end this evil reign. WE are going to attack the Devil and rid the earth of evil," I exclaimed.

You could have heard a pin drop, again. They looked at me like they were waiting for the punchline. Then you began to hear the chatter. The rumble grew to a whisper and a whisper to a conversation. Pretty soon that conversation was loud enough for the earth to hear us. I said,

"Gentlemen, Gentlemen......ask me. Give me your thoughts."The heavens were quiet once again. I stood there staring at them and they at me. Suddenly a voice rang true, "CAN I COME UP THERE AND TALK TO YOU?" I looked trying to find where this voice was coming from and said "YES...please come up." I saw a Defender making his way to me. When he appeared from the ranks this Defender was tatted from head to toe. Stocky big guy and bigger than most of the defenders. Good looking kid with almost all white feathers. He said "Shep...My name is Samuel; I like you left earth too early. I left my mother and my sister whom I love very much and look down on every day. I left them without being able to say goodbye. I hear my sister speak to me every day in her thoughts and watch a tear fall from my mother's face time and time again. I tell you this because there are many of us up here with families that just need to know that we are good. They need to know we are fighting to make sure they have a path to heaven. I believe I can speak for everyone here if I may. WE WILL FIGHT......we will never stop or refuse to fight. We were made for this shit. I would ask of you this. When we beat THAT.....DEVIL'S.....ASS (a quiet roar came from the defenders)....................I would like to hug my sister one more time so she feels my arms around her tightly like we did every time we saw each other. And I want to kiss my mother's forehead softly to tell her, I love her. I want them both to know "I AM GOOD" and I am kicking ass up here just like I did on earth. I not only ask this for me but for the thousands up here like me that we can give just some signal that points to the heavens for our loved ones to be at peace."

I stared at this guy for a good minute. I turned my head and looked over my shoulder at Michael. He gave me a nod of agreeance as I saw Raphael smile from ear to ear. I turned back with a smile on my face and in a low tone almost a whisper said, "Hooyah!" ......AND THE HEAVENS ERUPTED HOOOOOOOOOOOOOOOYAH!!!! I then held my Trident high for all to see and said "GENTLEMEN..................MAKE READY!!!!!!"

XXII

We trained hard over the next few weeks and sent many low-level recon missions to earth to find the best way we could lure the Suhtan from the school to get a good look at it. We believed the devil's lair is under the school; but until we can get those guys away from it, we could not be clear. I worked tirelessly with the Brigade Commanders on their task and each and every step of where they needed to be. They in turn worked with their men. We took on a different approach when it came to this mission. Every pattern that we used was different now. Our approach to each of the Suhtan would be met with each branch of Defenders as a team. They would all work together when it came to taking on each level the devil had in defense. We would platoon each brigade in and out so that we were fresh with every move we made giving rest through the battle. Each Defender with a purpose and each Defender honing their skills to the absolute best it can be done. We could do this because our numbers far outweighed theirs. All was coming together when the Archs came to me and pulled me aside.

Shep, Raphael called me over. We need to talk about when we take the shot. Michael and Gabriel came over. There are certain things that must be in place for us to not only kill the Devil, but even take the shot. If we do not have a clear shot, do not force it. I said, "what do you mean don't force it?" Gabriel said, "if you do not have a clear shot at the Devil, do not throw your trident." I said, "talk to me, tell me what is going on." Michael said, "it is YOUR trident that has been chosen to rip the heart from the devil. Your middle spear is red." I said, "yes, please tell me why." Michael said, "not yet but in time. The Devil will know it is you, not only by your weapon but also by the dark feathers. Even though you have turned many of them to white, you still have the darkest feathers of them all. He will recognize this and seek you out. If you do take the shot, the three of us will have to finish him once you pull his heart from his chest. Do you understand what we are telling you?" I said "yes, you are telling me that this is a 12-step process and if it isn't perfect, we are all in danger." Raphael said, "something like that, so unless you are absolutely positive about the shot and your ability to make it…. do not take it."

As they walked away, I sat feeling defeated. I watched my men and all the brigades working so hard to get everything right and there was still a greater chance of not completing the mission than there was in actually being victorious.

Jacob and Jerry came over to me and they could tell something was up. Jacob said, "shep, you good?" I told them that I was just reworking our advance on how we are going to approach this that is all. Jerry then said, "Shep, we are a team here. Don't bare the whole load when we can carry our share." I smiled at them both and said, "go…get back to work, we have evil to kill. I'll let you know what I need……I promise."

The next day we took a low-level recon on the school in hopes to see if there was some way to penetrate and get in. We needed to get the Suhtan away from it long enough to look for a chamber that will lead us to the devil in his lair. We were holding up in the clouds to disguise ourselves just watching and going over their every move when about a hundred Suhtan separated from the school and took off north toward Los Angeles. I quickly looked at Jacob and said "we have to follow them. Something is up." We sent signal to the teams and we followed at a distance to see what they were up to. It was not long, and they were hovering over a gang violence shooting where it looked like three were killed and they were rounding up the souls of the evil ones involved. You could hear the screams from the gang member's souls as they fought from being taken to the dark. I immediately told the teams to ascend and debrief on what we saw.

When we returned to the heavens, I huddled my men and said, "did anyone catch what just happened?" They all nodded yes. One spoke up and said they break away to get the souls they need of evil humans. I said "EXACTLY!!!" Now, where are there always people getting killed over gang banging or drugs? One voice said "CHICAGO!!!" I snapped my fingers and pointed in his direction. If it took approximately 100 of the Suhtan to go grab 3 people from Los Angeles. It will take 2000 of them away every weekend to Chicago. We now have the hole we are looking for to get into the school. This weekend we plan on watching where the hole opens, and then we will make a plan to approach the school.

I was excited. This brought us one step closer to our mission and it was a huge step. I debriefed the Archs on what we have figured out and what our plans were for this weekend on Earth. They agreed and told me to be careful and let them know what we find. If we can get in and check the layout of the school and find the blueprints, we just might be able to find the chamber that leads us to the devil's lair. We had to get in in order to get in.

We devised a plan to have two Brigades over Chicago and one over the school in San Diego. We would just watch this time. We needed to see what kind of hole they made and how many of us were really needed in each spot. I also told the brigades over Chicago that there are always innocents killed each weekend too. Make sure we grab them to protect them from the Dark. Many times, there will be children that are shot and killed in these violent attacks and we need to make sure that evil does not get to them before we do.

We descended on the school disguised in the clouds. We watched just far enough to be out of sight. We did not need the Suhtan to catch wind we were there with two brigades thousands of miles away. It was amazing how we could communicate up here by just speaking to each other no matter how far apart we were. We obviously did not have "radios" to communicate with but, just using a normal tone of voice and stating names we could talk to each other. It was nice when we had to separate the Brigades for any reason. We watched the school and about an hour in just as we thought about 2000 Suhtan headed east toward Chicago. I told Jerry who was commanding the Brigades over there that he would have company soon and to stand by.

With this amount of Suhtan departing it left many holes that we could get into the school now. I told the guys to watch and make a mental image of what it looked like and we would go over our mission when we returned to the Heavens. I made sure that Jerry saw everything he needed, and he told me that there were two children that were killed, and he was bringing them back. All I could think about was their parents and when I had to tell Lisa (Jacob's mother) about her loss. How can humans be so nonchalant about death? How do they randomly decide to shoot someone over property that is not even theirs? There is a glitch in some humans and unfortunately due to their bad decisions, some innocent become collateral damage. I told Jerry very well and we will give them safe passage to Heaven. I could not help but think of my Gesa at such a young age. The children are innocent. They do not know what or why. They are supposed to be taught by humans that have the knowledge just as those humans were taught when they were children. They do not know to be angry or dislike someone for color, religion, or belief system. It amazes me how humans take children for granted as if they were never one themselves.

As we got back to the heavens, we all met up and went over each, and every detail we saw. We matched the holes with the blueprint of the school and noticed the middle of the school had the most density in the population of Suhtan. This is where the cafeteria was. It was the largest room in the school, and it all made sense to me now.

We began to make a mockup of the school applying any, and all problems that we might encounter. As on earth, we went over and over it again and one more time for good measure. We did not need to use doors or entryways. Defenders could just walk through walls or obstructions to get to where we were going. The "problems" I am talking about are the Suhtan or any kid that has the evil in them that would be able to let others know we are there. We could literally fly over the humans and unless they had the evil, they would not even know we were present.

A week had passed in what seemed like minutes and again we were at the school camouflaged by the clouds and where there weren't clouds we formed them in the sky so it would look normal if anyone or thing looked up. We did not want one massive cloud above the school. That would kind of give us away now, wouldn't it?

This time we had the brigades over San Diego in hopes to catch a break and get in. We saw a mass of Suhtan break free and head southeast. I had a scout team follow with safety trailers to relay any alarms. We needed to know where they were going this time and how long we had. As they left, the holes started to appear. There was a huge gap in the back corner of the school by the baseball field. I told Jacob "that's our target." Jacob grabbed about 10 guys and we started to make our way down ever so gently as to not be noticed.

The approach was uneventful almost to the point it made me worry, but we made it to the ground and were entering the school. Being the weekend, we were free to roam without any students inside. We were careful to not make noise and to clear every room prior to moving to the next one. We had just cleared a room and all of us were in the hall when the custodian came around the corner whistling and mopping the floor. WE ALL FROZE. We watched for a minute and then he looked up from the floor he was mopping, and his eyes got as big plates. We heard him say "HOLLLLLLLLLLLLLLLLLY SHIT." I looked behind us to see what he was looking at. I could see him start to fumble with his mop. He then slammed the mop head against the locker breaking it off. He took a battle stance and I could see him shaking. "WHAT DO YOU WANT?" he yelled. I looked around to make sure I was not missing something. If I did not know better....... this guy could see us!!!! I started to slowly walk toward him. He tried to stand his ground, but he slowly backed up as I got closer. I was within 10 feet of him and he was looking right at me and his eyes would only break away for a split second to see my team's movement. I calmly asked, "can you see me?" He said "of course I can see you. Can you see me scared to death about to pee my pants?" He was a tall black man well-built and not too old. His hands were not hard as to think he had been working labor all his life and his speech had a hint of French Creole. So, I am quite sure this guy thought we were the Rougarou (roo-ga-roo).

(This was a mythical creature from the bayous in Louisiana, that was like western culture Big Foot, but much meaner and actually attacked livestock. Some of the French Creole say it is real and have had encounters with it.) I told him we were not here to hurt him. I asked him to describe us just to make sure he saw us as we are. He said, "describe you? Let's see, big as shit white boys that are ten feet tall and muscles all over the damn place and you are carrying pitchforks. And you want me to believe you are not here to hurt me?" I laughed, but I understood. I said, "these are TRIDENTS. We were all Navy Seals when we were on earth." Then I asked him what his name was. He said it was Julius Clemmons, but we could call him "Juice." I said, "ok Juice, my name is Shephard and you can call me Shep. These are my men and we are Defenders of Heaven." He then said, "did you guys take a wrong turn?" Jacob then said, "I like this guy." I motioned him into a classroom where I asked him to sit down. "Juice…. how can you see us?" He then told us how he was born with a veil over his face (it is called a birth caul. Where a newborn is born with a piece of the amniotic sac over their face. Some believe it to be good luck and say those kids are gifted) I told him that explains a lot. I asked if he had seen anything else. He said, "YES, all the kids here are assholes with exception of a few. Parents these days raise coddled little punks who think they can have anything they want for free. It is amazing how they disrespect me and the teachers… IT'S LIKE THEY HAVE NO UPBRINGING AT ALL…. RAISED IN A BARN IS HOW WE SAY IT!!!" He was laying it out and I had to slow him down. I raised my hands and said, "no…no…not like that. Have you seen anything abnormal here?" He looked around with his big eyes to see if anyone is around and he said "evil. I have seen lots of evil." "What do you mean," I asked? He said, "there is a cloud over the school. I see black creatures that look like they are in such pain roaming the halls with the kids. I act like I do not see anything and sometimes walk right through them. I do not want them to know I know. Some of these kids have one with them all the time." I told him, "We think this is a breeding ground for evil and maybe the devil's new lair." He was like "ohhhhhhhhhhhh shit. I am outa here," as he got up to walk away. I said, "no juice we need you. Will you help us. Can you take us to the cafeteria?" He said, "yes but can I have one of those pitchforks. I told him, "in time my friend, in time." He then got up and motioned us to come with him. He told us that the black creatures do not come in when the kids are not here as we were walking down the hall. I told him they were called the Suhtan. He said, "sooton, crouton I do not care, they scare me." Jacob hit my shoulder laughing at what Juice had said. Jacob said in my ear, "did he just call them a salad crouton?" I had to keep myself from laughing out loud. Juice then opened the door to the cafeteria and said here we are. He held the door as most of us just walked through the wall and you should have seen the look on his face when we did that, but he did not say a word. We looked around and it was normal. How could this be the place that is the epicenter of evil for this school? It looked normal. Something was wrong and it did not add up. Why would the Suhtan be so condensed over this spot? I asked Juice "do all the rooms look the same throughout the whole school? Same tile, same paint, was there anything out of the ordinary anywhere?" He said, "no they are all about the same except about a month ago the principal painted his office RED." I said, "take me there immediately." He ran down the hall and we were in tow. He scrambled for his keys to unlock the door and when he opened it you could almost smell the evil. The principal was infected and probably placed in a position of authority and was going after the kids. The room was deep blood red and his desk was as black as you could get wood to turn. I saw Juice standing in the doorway in awe. My guys were looking over every inch. THEN…. something slammed against the window. THEY SEE US…. the Suhtan saw us in the window and they were throwing themselves against the glass trying to get to us. I barked, "MEN SOUND THE ALARM." I looked out the window and I could see the clouds break as thousands of Defenders formed a net-like dome over the school many ranks deep. The black cloud started to rise to the sky and that was our key to get out. I told my men, "get in the fight." I turned to juice and said, "no time to explain but you are coming with me." I grabbed him by the arms and told him to hang on to me. I wrapped my arms around him and my wings the same as to hide him as we took to the skies. The battle was fierce, and I barked "ascend to the Brigades." We could not cleanse with this many evil in one place, so I did not want to have too much blood hit the earth. We flew about a mile away from the school where I put Juice down on the ground. I told him, "they didn't see you. So, you will not be in any danger. I am going to need a favor from you."

He was a little shaken, but nodded his head and said "ok, what?" I need you to keep an eye on this kid, as I showed him a picture of Blaine. I need to know where he goes, and how many times he goes to the principal's office. Can you do that for me?" He said, "yes." I told him I would be back in touch shortly, but we had to go before an all-out battle took place. "See you soon my new friend."

He watched until he could not see us anymore and I called for a damage report as we ascended to the heavens. All Clear and accounted for I heard Jerry call out. We have a new ally on earth, but I am not sure that is how the Archs are going to see it.

As we returned to the skies, we saw the Suhtan retreat and resume their hover over the school. We needed to end this reign of terror and it needed to be fast. I had to meet with the Archs when we got back up and I was not looking forward to it.

Jacob and Jerry were with me when I entered the room to speak with Raphael and Gabriel. Raphael said, "what did you see Shep?" I told him that the doorway to the lair is most likely in the Principal's office. I told him how he had recently redecorated for lack of better words and that you could sense evil as soon as you walked in. They were like "great!!! That helps us with our strategy good job." I said and then we were seen by a human. Gabriel slowly turned around looking straight at me. The glare from his face was amazingly stern. He said, "excuse me?" I told him that the custodian, who was born with a caul saw us. We did not know he was even there. Then Gabriel blew his lid. "WHAT DO YOU MEAN HE SAW YOU? DID

YOU SPEAK TO HIM? DID YOU EVEN TRY TO HIDE SHEP? WHY IS IT THAT ITS ALWAYS YOU THAT HAS THIS KIND OF STUFF HAPPEN TO HIM? DO YOU JUST ATTRACT THIS STUFF? IT IS NO WONDER THAT YOUR FEATHERS WERE ALL BLACK AND GREY. Sometimes Shep, I think you are more of a liability to us than you are an asset." I said, "really Gabriel? Should I take the blame for taking my men into a school that was supposed to be empty and accidentally stumbling on a human that JUST HAPPENED to be born with a caul and could see us? Do you really think I planned this out?" He barked, "NO!! THAT IS JUST IT. I DON'T THINK YOU PLAN ANYTHING OUT AND JUST FLY BY THE SEAT OF YOUR PANTS." Raphael stepped in and said, "let's just take a breather. Shep, what happened with the custodian" he said?

His name is Julius or Juice for short. He not only sees us, but he sees them. He does not let on that he sees them to protect himself. He told me that they just recently started appearing and that some of the Suhtan have picked certain kids and are with them all the time while they are there. Gabriel said, "it's a breeding ground." I said "exactly. They have chosen their future earth leaders and are going to make sure they are infected if not already." Gabriel walked back and forth with his hands behind his back. He was in thought and I was not going to say a word. He then said, "Shep, What's the plan?" I then inappropriately said, "hang on, let me check the seat of my pants." This was an ill-advised move that was not taken lightly as you could see Gabriel's head turn beet red. I am fairly sure that I added some black feathers back to my wings on that one. I held my hand up at him as a symbol of apology and acceptance that I had bad timing on humor. I told him that I was going to sit with Juice and pick his brain if permission be had. I said, "we will do it away from school for the least amount of danger." Gabriel looked at Raphael. Raphael then stated, "it can't hurt as long as all precautions are met." "VERY WELL," Gabriel barked. "I want to know a time and place and I am coming with you."

The very next weekend we went on another low level over the school. This time the Suhtan did not leave to go to any disturbance in any state. I can only imagine that they now know what we are doing here or have been told to stand guard. We watched Juice leave for the day, and we followed him home. We entered his home as he was getting out of his car. His wife and two daughters were there, but they could not see us. He walked in and saw 10 Giants standing in his living room and almost went into a what looked like a full-on seizure we scared him so badly. We did not say a word. His wife jumped up and asked if he was ok. He said, "I'm fine baby I just slipped coming in the door. As he fumbled around putting his stuff away, he kept looking at us. I motioned to him pointing to myself and then outside and he gave me a nod. I motioned for the men to go outside as I heard him tell his wife he was going for a quick walk. He would be right back. I saw him kiss his girls on the head and headed out the door.

"WHAT IN THE HELL ARE YOU TRYING TO DO IN THERE? GIVE ME A HEART ATTACK?" He exclaimed. I said, "I apologize, but we did not remember you telling us that you had a family and we were already in by the time you opened the door." He just shook his head. "Can we have a talk with you," I asked? He said, "yes... walk with me." As we walked slowly in his neighborhood, I wanted to know more about him. In the Military we learn interrogation techniques that are of value in everyday life. Some of these techniques were abrasive. Some were to just find out what kind of person we were about to trust with intel. I used them when I met my wife, having studied these techniques that were used on informants prior to joining the military. Knowing some were going to be used on me during training, I wanted as much of the edge as I could. When I ask someone a question about 20% of that is to find an answer. The other 80% is to see HOW they answer and if they question back.

When I wanted to see if my wife was interested in me when we first went out, I asked a series of questions. What is your favorite color? When is your birthday? Simple questions for sure but, not really wanting to know the answer. I wanted to see if she would answer, then ask me the same showing she was interested in MY favorite color or birthday. This way I would know she has a caring heart or is interested. When someone just answers what you ask them.... they are not interested in you so move on. So, I asked Juice some questions first to get acquainted and to know what to expect as we moved forward. My guys spread out around us as we sat on the curb guarding if anything came upon us. It was nighttime so we were hidden from evil for the most part, but I told Juice to talk softly so no one would think he was crazy and talking to himself.

How long have you been married Juice? He said she was his high school sweetheart. He could not keep his eyes off her in school. You could see him smile as he spoke of his wife. "She was the most beautiful woman he had ever seen. I was an outgoing guy Shep. I talked to everyone and had confidence when I did. But her, (he hesitated) It was hard to talk to her, and when I did, it did not come out very well. It was like my mouth would dry up and my tongue got really thick or something and that is when I knew I loved her." I smiled at him in awe of this love. "How old are your kids," I asked? He said, eight and ten." "You have a beautiful family," I told him. He then said, "Thank you very much. "I am blessed Shep." He then asked, "Do you have kids?" He then corrected himself and said "shep, I apologize. I didn't mean" and that is when I said, "it is ok Juice. I understand. Yes, I have a daughter and a beautiful wife. Thank you for asking. My daughter is a senior at your school and about to graduate." He said, "you are kidding me, what is her name?" I said, "Gesa" as I had to hold a tear from breaking loose. Juice looked at me and said, "I KNOW GESA!!!" He got excited and said, "I should have known she had a military dad." I asked, "why would you say that?" He then said, "Gesa is always polite and says hello to me every time she sees me. She always asks how I am and laughs because I call her "Miss Gesa. It is a southern thing," he said. "I'm from Biloxi, Mississippi." I smiled with pride. He said, "you did well." I told him, "unfortunately I left earth when she was three years old, so her mom is the one that deserves that badge. But thank you and that makes me proud that she treats you so well." I then looked at him and changed my posture a little and said, "Juice, you don't come across as a custodian type." He said, "I have not been doing this long. I have spent my whole life in sales. I have done very well in my life and have made many companies a ton of money. I left that all behind giving up on thinking that companies actually care about their employees. I used to think that the saying "you are just a number" was not true and found out the hard way. I got tired of companies telling me "this is our culture," as he held his hands above his head. Then to find out "their culture" is 200 feet below shit and no one cares about you when sales are down. You are a hero when you are the top salesperson, but when your sales are down, they are ready to move on to the next new hire instead of cultivating and proper training like they did back in the day. Working as a young man, companies wanted to keep you and invest in you. These days, they honestly do not even want to know your name. So, I left, and I am writing a book and working on some ideas I have. I would love to come up with the "next big thing," make my family proud and be able to help others that are struggling." He stopped and I could see it was hard on him. I put my hand on his shoulder and said, "your ethos is amazing. Do not ever change that, trust me. You want all the white feathers you can get," as I chuckled. "Juice, I would like to ask for your help if you are up to it?" He looked right at me and said, "if you honestly think I can help, I will give you all I can." I smiled and said, "thank you."

As I talked to Juice, I came up with a plan on how he would be notified that we were coming and that a great battle was going to take place. I needed him to get as many kids as far from the school as he could when he gets my signal. I did not tell him to concentrate on getting Gesa out. I did not want him to focus on one, but many. I needed to get as many kids out as possible as to not have them infected. He understood and I went over all of it with him. This would be a major role and a huge help to us. We did not need any more collateral damage and we did not need any more "Blaine's." I asked him where he wanted us when we came down as to not give him a heart attack again and he said, "now that I know you might be coming at any time just sit with my family and protect them until I get home if you are coming." I told him "consider it done."

I ended our talk with a firm handshake and a good feeling we do truly have an ally on earth. The battle is coming soon, and I pray Gesa will keep her head when it does.

XXIII

We were almost ready with our plan to attack the school. We thought it wise to send some kind of signal that we were coming. We wanted the first layers to know we were coming in advance to see how they set themselves up. The Archs were not too fond of giving the element of surprise away, but this strategy has been used for years on earth with the special forces of all nations.

The British once sent toy boats down the river in a battle that said, "we are coming." Not only did this mentally incapacitate their enemy from thinking clearly, but it also gave away their position as they moved "into" position. Very ingenious if you ask me.

We needed another low level and we had to talk to Juice. Our time was almost here so we had to make sure all was in place. We could not mess up and put our men in jeopardy.

I took Jacob and Jerry to go see Juice one last time to go over the plan before we attacked. Juice was up for the task and wanted to help in any way he could. I said "Juice, you told me that the Suhtan have picked some of the kids and they are with them all the time. He said, "yes, they follow them around all day." "Good," I said. "I need you to tell "those kids" that the angels are coming tomorrow. Look only at the child and not at the Suhtan. The Suhtan will hear you and they will then send a signal to the Devil." You could see Juice starting to sweat a little. I asked him. "are you going to be able to do this, we need you?" He said "Yea Shep. It is just when you said "Devil" the realization of how big this is has hit me right in the gut. Can you guys pull this off?" I told him, "we have a good plan of attack and we think we will be victorious." He said, "then count me in. What day do you want me to tell the kids and I will get it done?" I told him, "today is Sunday......Tuesday we will attack. Tell them Monday, as to not give the Suhtan too much time to plan but just time enough." "Will do Shep," Juice said. "How will I know you are coming," he said? I told him, "you will see the clouds move quickly and heavens trumpets will sound." He stared at me for a minute and then looked to the skies. He then turned to go back into his home and stopped and turned back to us. "Shep?" He called out. I turned and he said "if I don't see you again.... like......if something happens to you." I stopped him and said, "I will see you soon my friend." He kind of half-ass smiled but you could still see the worry on his face. It is not often you just meet someone, and they care that much about your wellbeing. We need more of this in the world.

XXIV

Back in the heavens, I met with the Archs including Michael. We went over the plan and over it again. All of them agree that we should be victorious in eliminating many Suhtan with this plan of attack, even if we do not get a shot at the Devil. We needed to protect our men and make sure we all came home. Michael said, "I'll call the brigades, let us get them up to date."

Monday came and for us up here we don't really keep track of days, but being that we had a human involved and they do, it was important for us to know what day it was so we attacked on the right day. Michael had called the Brigades and the heavens had Defenders as far as the eye could see encircling us as Michael began to speak.

"Gentlemen,

Tomorrow you will embark on the largest battle the heavens have seen. We will once again go on the offense and Attack Evil. Some of you have been here long enough to remember what happened last time we did this. For some of you, this will be your last battle. Not because of death or capture, but this battle will take the last bit of color from your wings ensuring your safe passage to heaven. You will have paid your dues. For others, this will be your first. Stay close and fight with everything you have. It will not be easy. Thank you for being such an instrumental part of our quest to rid evil from the universe. This battle will be a turning point. If all goes well and we are victorious it will set the ball in motion for evil souls on earth to be cleansed. If we are not successful, the ramifications are unknown."

I stepped up with Jacob and Jerry by my side. "Gentlemen, this is the plan." I went over it step by step with what we might see and where we are to be. I chose who did what and when they would be put in place. It was very intricate, so each defender needed to know his place.

I told the Brigade Commanders to split off and go over every detail of the plan with their Brigade. It was particularly important they knew their place.

I turned to Jerry and said, "go my friend, your Brigade needs you and I will see you soon." As I watched Jerry walk away, I turned to Jacob and just looked at him. He stared at me for a minute and said "do not doubt yourself. I can see it in your face. Be confident in your leadership. We have a good plan." I could only look at him and smile. What a great leader he has turned out to be and even though not on earth, but the most important place he could have become one…. he did. This made me proud.

I reached up and messed his long curly locks up and laughed. As I turned, I found an opening and searched for my wife. She was outside reading a book on the porch. She loved to read, and I think that it was kind of a way to get away from this everyday world for her. I watched her and could remember her voice on the phone when I called her from the zert. "Hello...................... hello? Shep? Talk to me." I wish I could talk to her again and hear her voice before this battle. I needed her strength and power. I calmly stared down at her and said, "very much." I had to get rest. I was helping lead Heaven's Armies into battle tomorrow. A world without evil................ could it even happen?

XXV

Under the cover of early morning before the sun crested the curvature of earth, we formed ranks. The Brigade Commanders gave their report of all accounted for. I told the men to check their gear and check each other. "KNOW YOUR PLACES," I barked. You could hear chatter that started from a whisper to what was almost thunderous in no time. I said, "Gentlemen, Gentlemen, calm your souls and trust your hearts. Let not one of you have doubts. Be confident in your training, and in your fellow Defender." I could sense their anxiety as time was growing near.

I said, "Brigade Commanders ON ME!!!" They formed a circle and I wanted to go over their positions one more time. I wanted to make sure they knew their place to ensure no mishaps and no lost defenders. They all were set on their responsibilities. I then hung my trident into the middle of the circle hanging on to the shaft. Starting on my left Jacob put his on mine and the next and the next and so on.

I then stated "Strength in the gifts that have been bestowed on us by Almighty God, speed in our flight as we descend on evil, accuracy to our target of the tortured souls. VICTORY...... upon us in the end."

Each of the Commanders stared at me, I looked over their shoulders to see all the Brigades staring. I scanned the heavens just using my eyes to look at all of them. I hesitated and in the faintest of whispers "Hooyah," AND THE HEAVENS ERRUPTED WITH "HOOYAH." I looked over at the Archs that were in their battle gear, held my TRIDENT high and yelled, "GET IN THE FIGHT!"

ONE BRIGADE AFTER ANOTHER....... took formation and we were on our way to earth. Seven brigades deep descending to earth. If you can imagine each Brigade with thousands of Defenders descending on earth at an incredible speed. "SOUND HEAVENS TRUMPET," I exclaimed!!! We could see the school and there was an army of Suhtan waiting. Our speed sounded like thunder crashing across the sky. You could see children running from the school. Juice had pulled the fire alarm and all exits were full of children. I could hear the screams of the Suhtan get louder. "FLARE," I yelled as my teams flared their wings to break speed. Not to a halt, but just enough to let the Archers fly right through us for an uncontested shot. Arrows like tracers in the night lit up the sky like shooting stars. I heard Jerry above us yell "FLARE," and his Archers in his Brigades did the same. Back at speed, we passed the Archers and three Brigades formed what looked like the tip of the spear. We hit the school full speed and went straight through the principal's office floor. We were in the passage to the Devil's lair. Still, at full speed, the Swordsmen were on the outer formation of the spear as my teams and the spears men were inside protected by them. Twisting and turning through the cavernous walls the Suhtan tried to use their old tactics to flank us. We did not let them have their rest. As we shot through the caverns the Swordsmen were attacking the walls making sure that we kept speed and remained untouched. You could hear their bodies slamming into the Suhtan as they would plunge their swords into and through their hearts. The rock walls would explode with the force of the Swordsmen thrusting the Suhtan against them. Two Brigades then followed any Suhtan that tried to come in behind us. One Brigade held position in the Heavens with the Archers to assure that Heavens remained protected. There were two battles now. The one behind us with the Suhtan and ours approaching the Devil's lair. I said, "Gentlemen make ready." With this we all reared back with our tridents and spears. The heat was blistering. The caverns opened and we saw the Devil's three layers of protection fire up. I yelled, "RELEASE" as thousands of tridents and spears took path toward the Devil. I knew I only had limited time to find a hole with the Devil unprotected. Our attack caught them a little off guard with how fast we came in. All you could see was our weapons in flight as it blackened the red walls of his lair. I watched as the tridents and spears struck their targets with an amazing amount of force. Some of the weapons were thrown so hard it ripped the Suhtans hearts right through their backs as the weapons exited their bodies. One by one I saw the Devil's protection fall.

My guys were ripping the hearts out of these creatures and there was no mercy. Moving from one evil hoard to the next these warriors were relentless with the task at hand. I looked desperately for an opening and there it was. I drew back and threw my trident with all my might. My aim was true and my flight on target. I could see the devil turning around. "C'mon, c'mon, c'mon," I said watching the flight of my trident. I had timed it exactly right. The impact would be exactly right when the Devil gets completely turned. Almost there......almost there and just as the Devil turned one of his protectors flew in front of my trident. He was hit with such force that the speed of the flight slammed him right into the Devil. The Devil grabbed my trident, ripped it from the Suhtans chest, and looked at the red center spear and FIRE CAME FROM HIS NOSE AS HE GROWLED!!! He looked up and straight at me. "YOUUUUUUUUUU," HE YELLED. I pointed at my trident and said, "I'm going to need that back asshole." He then reared back and threw it right at me. I dodged it as it almost hit me, and my trident went deep into the wall of his lair. He raised his hands in anger and screamed to the heavens. I yelled "MEN ON ME," as his protection had encompassed him once again. Break the wall down I need my trident. The men quickly made way of the wall as they broke the rock away from holding my trident. The noise was deafening as you could hear every scream of the Suhtan and every yell from the Defenders. The 4th brigade had flanked the Suhtan that tried to flank us, and you could hear the battle back in the tunnel. The blood of the evil was everywhere. Suhtan were all over the place but it was a fight we were ready for and they were not. The Devil's protection would not even let us get close. I tried to watch and see if there was a pattern. I wanted to see if there was any weakness but could not see one. Their patterns were so precise as to close any gap instantly that you think might be forming. How are we going to get to the evil one? Will we ever be able to pick his protection apart? We threw thousands of weapons at them and all were on target, but the devil's protection grew when we did. How was this possible and where were they coming from?

"MEN, ON ME!!!" My men instantly close ranks. "FIGHT WHAT YOU SEE" (meaning fight what is in front of you). I wanted them to concentrate on what was attacking them and since we were in closed ranks, we could keep track of each other better. I saw the 4th brigade coming through the tunnel and driving the Suhtan they flanked right at us. We were winning. We might be able to kill the first three layers of the Suhtan. I looked over my shoulder at the Devil and he stood and raised his arms and screamed. The sound was deafening. We all covered our ears and as we did the Suhtan retreated over us and they and the Devil disappeared. The cavern was silent. I looked around and said, "GENTLEMEN…STAND READY." I did not know what had happened and if they were going to surprise attack us again. It was silent and my gut was uneasy. "TO THE HEAVENS I YELLED!!!" Right as we started to the caverns to escape it was like an earthquake struck. The walls around us were coming down and the lair was crumbling in on itself. "GO, GO, GO," I yelled. We had to get out. It was dark and the direction of "out" was unknown. Twisting and turning through the winding caverns was almost dizzying trying to find the way out. The walls were coming down and three Brigades of Defenders were stuck in the Devil's lair. We were sitting ducks if we did not find our way out soon. We were about to be sucked into the earth and our souls would be devoured by evil. Suddenly a crystal blue light showed through the darkness and lit the way. "TO THE LIGHT," I yelled. "GO TOWARD THE LIGHT." We all flew as fast as we could as the earth was crumbling around us. We came shooting out of the school like we were fired from a cannon. Thousands of Defenders filling the sky like someone had kicked a hornet's nest. Michael was hovering over us with his sword held high. The blue hue was his sword showing us the way out. "TO THE HEAVENS," Michael commanded. Defenders from everywhere were now heading north. Jacob and I brought up the rear to make sure no one was left behind. The kids were gone, and it looked like they had all gotten out. We scanned the earth as we flew higher. You could see the blood of the evil had soaked into the ground as there was a sea of black around the school. It was slowly being sucked down into the earth by the Devil himself, to probably be used to infect other humans.

"JUICE!!! WE HAVE TO SEE JUICE," I exclaimed to Jacob. "TEAMS ON ME," I commanded to the skies and my teams gathered around. I saw Raphael hold his position. I spoke to him and said, "tell Michael we need to check on our human ally." He nodded and resumed his flight. I told my men "with caution we have to check on juice. We cannot give his position away or his family.

Make sure we are not followed and make evasive maneuvers in flight to look for any Suhtan on your six." "Aye Aye Shep." I had ten teams fly in ten different directions to make sure we were not followed. I did not want to put Juice or his family in any danger. We came upon his home and as we flew through the walls, he and his family were there...............AND SO WAS GESA!!!! I stopped in my tracks. She was playing with his small children. Juice just stared at me. I looked away from him as I was fixated on her. Was she alone or was Blaine here too? If Blaine were here, he would sense us, and we cannot have that. I looked around the room as Jacob went room to room to look. Jacob came back to the living room and shook his head. I could not take my eyes from her. I was just feet from my daughter. I wanted to hold her and touch her. My soul was screaming "HERE I AM GESA!!! DADDY IS HERE FOR YOU!!!" But I could not let her know I was here. My eyes went to Juice and my face was truly angry. I nodded my head toward the door as to say, "OUTSIDE NOW." Juice told his wife he would be right back. I was already outside waiting by the time he opened the door to come outside. He slowly opened the door as I saw him peek around the door with fear. I said get out here. He slowly shut the door behind him as he had a little limp. He said, "You do not look happy." I said, "HAPPY?? AM I SUPPOSED TO BE HAPPY? My daughter is ten feet from me, and do not get me wrong, thank GOD she is ok, but WHAT ARE YOU THINKING JUICE?" He hung his head and said, "I failed you shep." I looked at him and exhaled. In a calm voice I said, "Juice, you did not fail me or the heavens. You did an amazing job. You saved the children from evil. We owe you our gratitude." With his head still hung and looking at the ground he said "but?" I put my hand on his shoulder and said, "but nothing." I slowly turned and took a few steps away from him with my back to him I said, "when I saw Gesa my heart sank. My fatherly instincts kicked in and I wanted to hold her and protect her when I could not. I wanted to save her................ when you already had. Thank you, my friend." That is when he said "Shep, you should have seen her" with excitement in his voice. I slowly turned and saw a smile from ear to ear. He said, "Shep, she's your kid alright!!!" His energy level picked up and he was almost dancing with his arms going every which way as he told the story. He said, "when I hit that fire alarm, Gesa stood in the halls and barked orders to all the kids. "This side out that exit and this side out that one over there. You, you, and you clear the rooms and make sure NO ONE is left behind. LET'S GO PEOPLE, HELP EACH OTHER."

Juice was doing a jig. He said, "I've never seen ANYTHING like it." It was amazing. I smiled like a proud dad and tears rolled from my face. "She really did that?" I asked him. "As God is my witness," Juice said with his hand in the air as if he was swearing in the military. I looked at Jacob and he was grinning ear to ear. I quickly collected myself. I told Juice "thank you. You are a true ally and you did an amazing job. Will you please make sure Gesa gets home safe?" He said, "I sure will Shep. It was my pleasure to help you Defenders. I was scared to death I would mess it up." I shook his hand and watched him go into his house. I could see Gesa sitting on the floor with his kids as Juice opened the door. It was as if she looked past him into the street with a smile on her face. What was she looking at? Could she sense I was there or am I just wishfully hoping? Either way, I got to stand ten feet from my daughter. It has been 15 human years since I have been that close to her. Thank you, God, for letting me have that moment.

We ascended to the heavens as my teams stood guard as we passed and we as they passed. Each team taking their turn at altitude to make sure all of us got back north safely. I met with the Archs as I entered the heavens. I asked them for a damage report. Gabriel said, "surprisingly we have no casualties. Some defenders have torn wings and some cuts and bruises we came back as we left ......as one." "That is great news, I said. Our human ally on earth did a great job and we congratulated him." Raphael then said, "keep him close, we will need him again." I told him, "will do." Michael then came to me and said, "before I get back to my post, I want to thank you for a job well done. We eliminated thousands of the Suhtan. I would have liked to have cleansed the evil blood, but it would have been impossible to do where we were at." I told Michael, "thank you for believing in me and my team. The brigades were amazing, and the brigade commanders would love to hear the same from you. It would mean a lot to them." He nodded his head, told me he had to give a pass down to the big guy, and flew north to his post. Raphael said, "your men need time to rest and heal." I said, "thank you I will tell them." He then turned to me and said "Shep, you are needed, remember that" ....and he was gone. I turned to Jacob and said "tell the men to rest and we will debrief in the morning. I am going to check on my family."

I found an opening and saw my wife. She was making some dinner for Gesa and Gesa was telling her how part of the school caught on fire and they had to evacuate. "Mom, it was so cool. The fire alarm went off and I immediately started telling people what exits to go to and got help clearing the rooms. I wanted to make sure nobody was stuck, and we all got out. I was almost out when I looked back, and the kids had trampled on Mr. Julius. He was laying on the floor with a hurt leg. I ran over to him and helped him up. I wanted to make sure he made it out. He has a little limp, but I think he is going to be ok." My wife was just listening to her with her arms propped up on the counter. I looked around like, "he didn't tell me that part." I was amazed at my daughter's ability to focus during the pandemonium. She is her daddy's girl, but her mom has been training her more than I knew.

I sat for hours and for all I know it might have been days. How did we not penetrate the Devil's three layers? I was beside myself that with as many weapons we threw at him that no one got to him. I was going over and over it in my mind and the more I thought about it the further from a solution I got. I just knew we were going to get him but being my first meeting with him I can tell you this, he is not stupid and his strategy strong. Where were the three layers coming from to replenish the ones we killed? It is puzzling to me. I needed rest and maybe I could concentrate better. But if I rest will I forget what I saw? My head was scrambled eggs and my adrenaline was depleted. My eyes felt heavy, so I laid back and just looked up at the universe. Next thing you know.... I was asleep.

"YOUUUUUUUUUUUUU" as loud as thunder shook me as I woke up startled dreaming of the Devil looking right at me and saying that. I grabbed my Trident and looked closely at the red middle prong. How did he know it was me and who I am? Why is my middle prong red" Why do I have one red feather in the dead center of my wings? I would ask the Archs but all they say is "in time Shep, in time." And THAT does not answer much no matter what the questions are. I jumped up to shake off the sleepiness. I slept through the morning and into the afternoon. My guys were training, and Jacob saw I was awake and came over to me. He said, "Shep, you were OUT!!! That battle took it from you didn't it?" I said, "it must have Jaker. Did you and the men get to rest?" Jacob said, "yes, the men are waiting for debriefing." I told him to give me a minute and bring them over. I went to a clearing to make sure my family was well and saw a letter from Gesa

Dad,

Tonight is my graduation, and all I can think about is how you being there would be the coolest. I imagine you will be in some form and in my heart. Mom will be there, and she is letting me carry a picture of you in your dress whites as I get my diploma. I do not know where you are, but I am guessing in heaven. I hope that you are proud of me. If you can or if you are allowed to look down, because I do not know how it works up there, I hope you are watching me tonight. Watch what I do when I get my diploma. I am going to send you a message. I hope you like it. I love you very much and miss you.

~Gesa

Again, my heart sank. I had planned on being there for everything she did, and this graduation was a huge part of it. It is so hard for me to live in death, watching her grow up and not be a part of her life or share all the good with my wife. Rhonda (my wife) has done an amazing job with her and I could not be prouder. She is as strong as I thought she would be if not stronger and I was excited for her and worried the same. Her and Blaine seemed to be getting more and more serious by the day. I am not sure what path he will choose once sports are over for him, but he will be under a watchful eye every step of the way...........MINE!

My men started to muster around me for a debrief. I said men how are we feeling today? About 10,000 answers came out and I did not catch one of them, so I just said "GOOD, that is what I like to hear." Jacob just laughed because he knew.

I debriefed the men on the good and bad from our battle. We went over every step and in some instances, we role-played how we did it and how it should have been done. Showing the advantages and disadvantages of the battle. I told them that they were near flawless, and I had never seen so much intensity in any battle both Defender and when I was human. I thanked them for getting in the fight and how they knew not to leave anyone behind. "Rest now," I said. I want you to stop training for a few days and recover both physically and mentally. We need to stay clear. Just remain watchful in case needed. "Aye Aye," came from my men. They disbursed, I told Jacob I was going to watch Gesa's graduation and asked if he wanted to come. We found a clearing as my heart filled with pride. I could see my wife in the stands dressed so elegantly. She always knew how to turn heads when she went out and a class act with the way she dressed. She was stunning. She had laid what looked like a brochure next to her as if she were saving a seat. I looked down at it and it was a guest pass with the name "Shephard" on it. Tears filled my eyes and then they let loose as I wept uncontrollably. I felt Jacob's hand on my shoulder calming my emotion. The love my wife has for me is BEYOND my comprehension. I thought back to when we went on our first date. I ordered something I had never tried. She ordered her favorite dish. She would talk about how much she loved this dish and she was so looking forward to eating it again. As our server set our plates down you could see the smile radiate from her face like a beacon to the whole restaurant how happy she was. We started to eat, and I took two bites and pushed it away. She looked at me and said, "what's wrong?" I told her, "that is horrible." She immediately grabbed my plate and hers and swapped them. She said, "eat mine, I will eat this one." A LOVE SO GREAT TO GIVE UP YOUR FAVORITE FOOD WITHOUT HESITATION!!!!!! WHO DOES THAT? If it were me, I would have said "well let's order you something else." My greedy ass would have eaten my favorite food. GOD HIMSELF would have had to intervene on that one, but she did it without thought or prejudice.

I cleared my face and found Gesa on the football field in her seat. I could see my picture with her and some paper under it face down that I could not read. The ceremony was starting. We listened to every speech from the valedictorian to the principal. I was watching the principal closely knowing he had been infected. The guest speaker was some gazillionaire and his speech was actually kind of good. I noticed that he looked in one spot most of the time when he was emphasizing anything. I looked at that spot trying to find what it was and what kid. IT WAS BLAINE! Did he and Blaine know each other and if they did how? I watched more closely now at Blaine's reactions when anyone spoke. They started to call out names in alphabetical order as the kids walked to receive their diplomas. I watch what looked like 800 kids in this graduating class walk one by one to the podium. Most of them had honor tassels which was quite amazing these days with the dumbing down of our school's education system. Then I saw Gesa stand as it was her rows turn. I could see the excitement in her face. She looked so grown up. It was a proud papa moment for sure. As she was next to get her diploma, I hit Jacob on the arm and said here it comes. She shook hands with her instructors and got her diploma. She took about four steps and I saw her unzipping her graduation gown. When she dropped her gown, she had US NAVY CAMO on. She donned her NAVY cover and saluted her mother. She unfolded that piece of paper and she held it high for the world to see. It said US NAVY RESERVE!!!! I looked at Jacob and I was speechless. My little girl was going to be a US NAVAL OFFICER. I did not know what to say.

I looked at her mother and she had tears in her eyes as she scanned the skies like she was talking to me, hoping I saw this. I just stared down at them in awe. My Gesa is going to be a Naval Officer. A proudness came over my soul. I would have never imagined. I was excited and scared at the same time. With her strength, she will do fine. She kind of danced off the stage with her arms in the air. Blaine was waiting for her at the end of the ramp and she jumped into his arms with excitement. Then I saw him look to the skies like he was trying to find something, and Jacob put his hand on my shoulder. "His strength is growing Shep." I just stared at him in anger as I saw a grin on his face. He kissed Gesa and they walked off together.

I turned and walked about 10 steps. "HOW DO I STOP HIM JACOB? HOW DO I INTERVENE IN THEIR RELATIONSHIP? (as I paced back and forth) THERE HAS TO BE A WAY!!!" Jacob just listened as I went on a full-fledged rant over this guy. On earth, I was the one that preached about breeding calm, and yet now, I am going nuts and Jacob is the calm one. There had to be a way to put a wedge in their relationship. I had to ask the Archs if there was anyone that had knowledge of how. I had to get him away from Gesa. She was in danger and did not even know it.

As I walked from the clearing I stopped and turned to Jacob and told him I had to get some rest. I had to clear my head. I needed to talk to the Archs. A mind without knowledge is confused when it thirsts for it. I had to get as much information as I could in order to do this right. Blaine was a spreader and I needed to find out how the guest speaker played a role in Blaine's life. There was so much I had to do, and I wanted to know now. I HAD TO KNOW NOW. I ran back to the clearing to find my wife. She was gone. I searched the stadium for her, but I could not see her. I searched where she was sitting and all that was there was my guest pass with the name Shephard on it. But now there was something written under my name. I looked closer. "VERY MUCH" is what it said. A calm came to my soul. My wife was leaving me a signal for that "just in case" he can see it moment. I mouthed "very much" back to her wherever she was. I will check on them in the morning to make sure they are ok.

XXVI

The next morning, I woke up to the guys cheering each other on and it was loud. I know earth could hear us but to them, it was a bad storm they were having. I went to see what all the fuss was about, and it was not just my guys. Jerry's swordsmen were there too, and they were having arm wrestling competitions between both teams. My first reaction knowing my men was this is not going to be good. Seals are savage competitors and if we lost (which we OBVIOUSLY never do) it would not bode well for the other team. Besides, the one who lost would get teased by his teammates for years to come. I stood and watched and just smiled. They were having a blast with each other and it was good to see them let loose and have good fellowship. Raphael came by and said, "shep, why are you not competing with your men." I looked at him and told him, "a leader has to be the strongest in his men's eyes. If for any reason I were to lose an arm-wrestling match my leadership would be compromised." He looked at me and said, "that is one way to think of it." I said, "one way? Is there another?" He then stared at me and said, "you are an amazing leader. Your men and the Heavens love you for your strength, but a leader is also humble and humbled at times. A physical weakness may show the vulnerability of the body but a good sport upon loss shows the strength of the mind." I just stared at him and he stared back at me and I said, "well, I am obviously humbled at what you just said and I may even write that down," as I gave him a shit-eating grin. He then asked me how I was holding up. I told him, "that my brain was scrambled and going in so many directions. Like how did we miss the devil? How did we let him get away? When will we get another chance at him? I am sure he will be in hiding for a while will he not?" I asked Raphael. Raphael said, "maybe, but he is smart and very meticulous. Sometimes I am sure we are the least of his worries. The Devil is more intrigued by slowly turning the humans against God. He does this in many ways, and in most instances takes earth years to achieve his goal, but he is relentless in his quest. Our main goal is defending Heaven. We must make sure Evil never rises otherwise all is lost."

I looked at the stars and every time I do, I am in awe. I said, "Raphael." He said, "yea Shep." I said, "what are the chances I can meet with Michael on a few personal questions?" Raphael said, "I will ask him and get back to you." I told him, "thank you and I would appreciate it if he did. Raphael then patted my shoulder and said, "I am glad you are here Shep. Not that I do not want you in heaven because I do, but you here gives these men hope." I then said, "how was that?" Raphael looked at my feathers and then he said, "because they all know they are going to make it to heaven before you do," as he gave me a shit-eating grin. I pointed at him and said, "you are good Raphael, I never expected humor out of you, but you pulled it off." He smiled and flew away to go see Michael. I stood there pulling my feathers around in front of me. After that comment, I wanted to see how far I have come. It was good to see some white in them finally, but I had a long way to go. I was here for the duration and my goal was to rid the earth of evil no matter how long I had to stay.

A blue hue of light lit up the skies. It was Michael coming to talk to me. Michael said, "Shep, you wanted to speak with me?" I said, "yes sir, if you have time." Michael said, "I always have time for my armies." He said, "walk with me." We started to walk, and I told him that "I don't know what I'm allowed to ask and not allowed to." Michael said, "ask anything you want and if I'm not allowed to answer, I will tell you.

"My mind is going 100 miles an hour with many things. I am trying to figure out our next attack and what to do for my men. I also want to know about my family. Is there a place in heaven for my wife?" Michael hesitated and said "Shep, there is a place in heaven for everyone when they are born. Especially the unborn that were not given the chance to live. They hold an incredibly special place in Heaven. Through life, Humans make decisions that hold their spot, jeopardize that spot, or in many cases lose that spot to never again regain it. That is the worst-case scenario and that is where the Devil gets most of the Suhtan from. God is very forgiving. Matter of fact he is the most forgiving. The Devil was once God's favorite angel. God gave him chance after chance to straighten up and stop trying to overthrow him per se. He would try to tempt God and he would exaggerate what "he" could do for God. Until one day God had enough, and he banished him to hell. Therefore, the Devil needs the earth to turn evil. It is the only way he gets power. It is kind of like an "I'll show you" kind of moment for him. God gave man his own free will. Humans inherently know right from wrong it is the ONLY thing that is identical in all the human DNA. Otherwise, every human DNA is completely different than anyone else's, even in the same families. This is one of the miracles God has given humans. They are all uniquely different from each other and not one the same. But to get back to your question. Your wife for one is a saint to have put up with you, as he nudged me with his elbow and smiled, but she has done well on earth. I am not allowed to tell you a definitive answer, but barring some catastrophic failure on her part to remain good between now and then, I would vote her in." I smiled and my heart jumped. Such good news, because I knew what a good person she is and how pure her heart is. This made me incredibly happy. I then said "Gesa, I know she is young, and the answer would probably be the same, but can I ask you to protect her? You know the situation she is in and it scares me. My way of handling things is not always the right way, and I am helpless when it comes to guiding her anymore." He looked at me and said, "those that call on my protection get it."

I then took a minute and said, "my father. I have tried to stave my anger for him, but it is the same up here as it was on earth. I have tried to forgive him, but I cannot get it to come from my tongue. It seems that all my memories are of the bad and I have forgotten any that might be good. I know in my heart that he was a good man. He was a great friend to his friends. Is he in heaven?" Michael stopped walking and looked at me and then hung his head. He turned from me and with a long pause, he started to speak. "I am not sure I am to tell you this or should my lips stop speaking at this moment. What I tell you about your father will be in strict secrecy. Not from God because he hears everything, but to the other Archs, your men, and any humans you might encounter on earth. You are a first for the Defenders of Heaven." I looked at him with unknowing eyes. "I am not sure I follow you, Michael," I said. Michael took a deep breath and said. "I have walked with your father as I do with you." My eyes grew wide. "I have had conversations with your father that mirror my conversations with you. He cried many tears and screamed in anger for all the heavens to hear him. His anger was not directed at you or your brother. He directed his anger at himself. He spoke of you and your brother and how he was too hard on you both. He thought he was preparing you the best he knew how. He admitted to always putting you second and sometimes even wishing you were not around at all." Hearing this brought tears to my eyes. It was like reliving my pain as a child. "He has cried many tears on our walks. He has told me about HIS father and how he vowed to never be like him but failed in so many ways. He has heavy regrets about your life Shep." Michael then said, "your brother tried to divert your fathers' anger from you onto him many times so that you could catch a break. You didn't know that, did you Shep." I said, "my brother did that for me?" "Yes, remember that time your brother came in late for curfew on Christmas?" I said, "ohhhhh do I remember that one." Michael grinned. He said, "your brother noticed that your father was giving you hell for weeks and wanted him off our back. So, he came in late for curfew so that your father's focus would change to him." "He was trying to save me," I said. Michael said, "one of many times shep. Your brother did not have it easy with your father either. Your father admitted that to me but getting back to the question. What I am about to tell you stays with us. Your father has not made it to Heaven yet. Nor is he in danger of Hell. Time will tell when he gets the nod to ascend. Each human that comes north toward the heavens still must make the right decisions as they did as physical beings on earth. Just pray for his peace Shep. If you are going to ask me next about your mother. Just know that she prays for more people and never asks for anything. She has a path much like your wife." I smiled.

"Lastly......my men. How can I help them get to heaven faster?" Michael smiled and said, "you amaze me in many ways Shep. Pick up your mess and we will talk soon." I looked down and there were five grey feathers at my feet. I looked back up and Michael was gone. I was at peace with my talk and it answered a few questions that I had about my family in an indirect way. My wife and daughter had a path and that is all I could ask. I knew they were strong enough not to mess that up and I would do anything in my power to help them along the way.

XXVII

As I approached my men to maybe get into a little competition the HEAVENS TRUMPET SOUNDED. My men came running as I saw the Brigades form. Raphael, Gabriel, and Michael all came in a hurry. "We have a black cloud coming north and its nothing we have ever seen. This cloud has blacked out the earth" Michael said. I barked, "STAND READY, STAND READY" as I heard the Brigades repeat down the line. I looked at Michael waiting for instruction. He said, "Shep, GET IN THE FIGHT." Immediately I turned and gave orders. "BRIGADES, EXPAND FORMATION! FOUR MAN TEAMS, FIGHT WHAT IS IN FRONT OF YOU!!!!! GET IN THE FIGHT AND LEAVE NO DOUBT!!!!" The Brigades expanded like a net around the earth as if it were a giant force field. Each section when attacked would close around the attacker. We were headed toward the black cloud as fast as we could fly. We needed to intercept it as far from heaven as we could. They had a start on us, so we were compromised on time. Hundreds of thousands of Defenders were headed to what would be the biggest battle the universe had ever seen. The Archs were in the lead with my teams to follow. I could see the black cloud was getting bigger and bigger by the second as we both got closer to each other. Our weapons gleaming in the sun and ready to strike anything and everything that dared to pass. I yelled, "ARCHERS AT THE READY DRAW!!!" I could hear them stretch their strings back as far as they would reach to get as much speed on the arrows as they could. Suddenly, the black cloud stopped just a short distance from us. I yelled, "FLARE, FLARE" as to put the brakes on in case this was a trap. Both the Suhtan and we were frozen in space. Hovering in time, no one was moving, and nobody said a word. "Stand ready men. Keep your eyes peeled, something is not right," I told them very quietly. The center of the Suhtan was as black as the color itself. They sat staring at us with so much pain. There was a movement from the center. I could not quite make out what it was, but it was big. Michael held his hand high to hold our position. I yelled, "MY TEAM ON ME!!!!" I wanted a concentrated group to be able to take whatever was coming out of that darkness to meet it head-on. My team was at the ready and my men were locked on target. Something was coming out of that darkness and it was not going to be good. "C'mon c'mon c'mon…. show yourself," I said in a quiet voice. I could see Jacob just itching to jump on anything that moved. I could see movement and I was trying to identify what it was. It was almost a jumbled movement. My eyes grew as I instantly saw the core. "IT'S

THE DEVIL!!!!! ON MY MARK" I yelled…. STAND READY STAND READY." The Archs immediately went to a battle stance and our side of heaven turned blue as Michael's sword gleamed as if it were the sun itself. The Archs weapons began to ring like water being rubbed around a crystal glass rim. The Devils three layers were coming out of the center of the Suhtan. Just as Michael was about to yell "ATTACK," a voice came from the center. It was the Devil. He said, "Michael, it is sad to see I got this close to your prize. I am sure you will be reprimanded if I allow you to go back. Look at you Gabriel, and you Raphael, like you are a match for me with your pathetic weapons. Look around at my men. Some of them were yours until you so poorly tried to take me on my terms. Would you like to donate some more today, or shall I just TAKE THEM?" I saw my men half lunge but holding themselves back until the command was given. "I am amazed that God still lets you command Heaven's armies. Pathetic to say the least, but then again, I should be the one you are protecting up there. How does it feel to be second best Michael? God's alternate choice?" Michael said, "It is a shame that you still believe that highly of yourself when you live in the dungeons where you belong. That YOU could have ever commanded anything righteous under God. Who lied to you and told you that you were actually worth God's time or energy? You talk a good game, but yet you still hide behind your three layers as we stand in front of seven." Just then the three layers stopped spinning and they slowly started to open like a rib cage being split right down the sternum. As they opened wider and wider, you could see two blood red eyes gleaming out in what looked like the center of hell. Slowly the eyes got closer and larger. In no time the Devil himself emerged from his three layers. The most grotesque creature you have ever seen. His skin was crawling with movement of what looked like millions of tortured souls. Without taking my eyes off him I said "Jacob, his skin, do you see it?" He said, "yes, it moves." I said, "good eye. This is how he was replenishing his three layers so quickly when we attacked him. They live on him like a parasitic disease on his body." The Devil walked out of his three layers and held his arms stretched to his side. "ANYONE? ANYONE WANT TO TRY ME?" he yelled. "DO ANY OF YOU HAVE WHAT IT TAKES TO TRY TO KILL ME? ARCHERS? DO YOU REALLY THINK YOUR PUNY ARROWS WILL PENETRATE MY SKIN? SWORDS AND SPEARS HOW CUTE the devil laughed. AND YOUR TRIDENTS ARE ALL BUT A MYTH SO YOU CAN FEEL STRONG AND MIGHTY. NONE OF YOU HAVE THE POWER NOR THE BALLS TO TRY ME..................or you would have already." I said in a low voice, "defenders at the ready, hold the line." "WHERE IS HE?" the Devil exclaimed. WHERE ARE YOU "CHOSEN ONE," SHOW YOURSELF TO ME." I stood ready and waiting on Michael's command. "I SEE YOU BEHIND YOUR LEADER CHOSEN ONE. YOU DON'T HAVE TO HIDE FROM ME. COME LET ME SEE YOUR FACE." I did not move. I just stood and stared right at him. "I WANT TO MAKE YOU A PROPOSITION CHOSEN ONE." The Devil's voice got calm as he said "come with me and command my armies. I will give you power beyond belief." I hesitantly took a step forward. I could hear Jacob call my name under his breath. The Devil smiled as he continued, "Command "MY" heaven and all of the earth. See your family whenever you want, and I will let you talk to them and guide them." I took a few more steps forward as my eyes never left his. I heard Jacob say, "Shep, you are not listening to this BEAST, are you?" The Devil continued, "I will let you hold your wife and kiss her again. She will feel your touch and she can be with you." Again, I took a few steps forward this time I was even with the Archs. I heard Michael say, "Shep, it is lies. Do not fall for this." The Devil continued, "I will let you kiss your daughter and protect her. I will let her have armies under her as she was born of greatness." I took a few steps forward never taking my eyes off his. I heard Raphael call out "Shep, snap out of it." I saw the Devil extend his hand and said, "come with me and I will give you all the lands to do with as you please. I will let you be the most powerful man on earth to form it how you wish. I.......... can give you this if you just take my hand." I stood still for a moment and I could hear my guys behind me saying "this can't be happening, Shep come back." I hear Michael tell the brigades to stand ready making sure they were listening for his word. "Come, the Devil said. Be the legend you were born to be, and all earth will kneel to you. Take my hand Chosen One and all this can become yours." I reached out with my left hand while carrying my trident in my right. The Devil said, "lay your weapon at your feet it is not needed here." I bent over to lay my weapon down slowly while still reaching for his hand. I looked down to place my Trident on the ground. As I did, I took a step with my left foot toward him to get the right stride, SPRUNG UP AND THREW MY TRIDENT AS HARD AND AS FAST AS I COULD IN HIS DIRECTION. I could see his three layers spin up and Michael yelled, "Archers RELEASE" as thousands of arrows took flight. My Trident was on track and the throw was true. Just as my Trident reached the Devil he reached out and caught it and laughed out loud for the universe to hear. "STRIKE TWO," he said as he broke my Trident over his knee and threw it to the ground. He yelled, "I WILL MAKE YOU PAY FOR THIS CHOSEN ONE. YOU WILL HAVE WISHED YOU TOOK MY OFFER" as he escaped into his three layers just as the Archer's arrows bludgeoned anything that moved. I yelled "Brigades release" as every Defender that had a weapon of flight released to kill whatever moved. The only light that could be seen was the light from Michael's sword. We had blacked out the sun with thousands upon thousands of weapons to kill these tortured souls. The black cloud started to retreat as the Archers reloaded and released again. The Swordsmen took a forward position to intercept any advance from the Suhtan as they retreated to earth. Michael commanded "Archers Guard" as they took a forward position in front of us all. Michael looked at me and I at him. I nodded my head as if to tell him I am good. His eyes at first with doubt, but I knew he knew that I was only trying to get a clean shot. He just had the look of "you should have told me first," but I did not have time. I walked over and picked up the pieces of my Trident and harnessed it on my back.

I made sure that the Devil had retreated a safe distance. I then barked "Cleanse" as we had killed many of the Suhtan upon the Archer's release and the Brigades counter release. We would be here for a while. As the blood of the evil suspended and we formed our funnel Jacob made way over to stand by me in the cleanse. He looked at me with a serious face and said, "don't ever do that shit again." I laughed and he said, "it isn't funny" and I laughed even harder. He eventually smiled that Jacob smile and started to laugh with me. I could hear the chatter of the brigades while we were in the cleanse as my name was on everyone's tongue. The Archs started heading north and I called out "Michael, I'm going to need another Trident" with a huge grin on my face. I saw him look at me and roll his eyes before he resumed his path up north.

The rain came down on earth in what almost caused flooding from the cleanse there was so much blood of the evil. It is nice to see fresh cleanse hit the earth and nourish it with hope instead of all the hate that is down there. When we were finally done, we called the Archers back north and as they ascended, we took turns taking our position to protect as we all moved up the ladder until we were at a safe altitude to travel together. As I traveled north, I did not say much and neither did my guys. They have surrounded me in a giant sphere of protection. I took in the beauty of the universe once more. I cannot imagine

anything more amazing with what I see up here. I wish we could share this with earth, but I believe it is one of the blessings we get for being chosen to come to heaven. It is worth it so far. If heaven is more beautiful than this.......
im going to lose my shit.

XXVIII

Back in the heavens, we debriefed on what we saw and if we saw anything that would help us next time we met the Devil. I thanked my men and apologized to them for letting them think that I was going to take the Devil's offer. I told them I would have shared my plan with them, but there was no time and I did not want them to interfere and possibly get harmed. They understood and some of them even said "we were going to bludgeon you ourselves if you had taken any more steps forward," as they laughed. I saw Jacob by himself just staring into the universe. I walked over to him and said "Jaker, you good?" He smiled and said, "that seems to be our question for each other huh?" As both of us laughed. He said, "yea Shep." He hesitated and turned to me and said, "I thought I had lost you man. I thought you were really being hypnotized by that son of a bitch and I had lost you." I said "Jaker, brother I'm sorry." He said, "I get it that you couldn't say anything and I would have done the same thing, but my heart sank, and

I felt the pain of what I think I put my mother through." A tear fell from his cheek and he said "Shep, will she ever forgive me? Does she think her boy was a quitter? I never wanted this pain for her. Feeling what I felt with you looking like you were going to leave and then realizing that her pain is a million times what I felt." He started to sob, and I stepped toward him. "I wish I could take it back Shep," he said. "I wish I could take that pain from her and have just known", and I stopped him there. I said, "Jaker, you were and still are a fighter brother. You were battling brother, and more times than not when we fight that battle as hard as we can, as humans, sometimes we lose in that situation. She knows you are not a quitter. She knows you did not mean her pain, and she understands yours. She knows what you went through. Your mom is an amaaaaaaazing woman. She is as strong as they come, but understand this, (I hesitated) She is going to wooooooooooooop that ass when she comes up here," as I smiled and held back a laugh with everything I could. He raised his head slowly looking at me with that serious look then started to laugh uncontrollably. "SHE IS ISN'T SHE?" he exclaimed as we were now both laughing uncontrollably. I was crying from laughing so hard. I gave him a big hug and just held him. This kid was something special and everyone he met knew it. Most of all God knew it and the minute he had the chance to grab him............ he did.

As the last ray of sun was going behind the arch of the earth I wanted to check in on my family. I found a clearing and sat for a minute just looking at the beauty of the planet earth. How perfect it seemed and how well made it was. Land for humans to live and enough of it they did not have to argue over. Water to nourish the land with such amazing plant life and wildlife. It is a wonder how anyone would ever believe that there is NO GOD. There is so much proof of it if they would just look around and clear their heads. We all take things for granted and I hope the humans come to realize what they have. But as long as there is evil, they will be swayed and tempted. They will be lied to that good is bad and bad is good and EVEN THOUGH THE FACTS PROVE IT, the weak will follow.

I looked through the clearing and saw my wife. I am more and more amazed at her beauty the older she gets. Not just her outer beauty, but her soul is like a beacon for me. I miss her. I looked for Gesa and she was not around. I did however find a letter on her desk.

Dear Dad,

Damnit I Miss You. How have you been? Anything exciting happen where you are? (I smiled knowing that the devil left earth just to tempt me) I survived boot camp and school. The NAVY is great. It is nice to be in the reserves where I can be close to home here on Coronado. This way I can still stay with mom and help her with anything she needs. She is good and still as beautiful as ever. I hear her talk to you sometimes. She is strong, but she breaks down from time to time because she misses you so much. I am just a few miles from where you trained for the SEALS. I went by the amphib base and they have a statue of the fallen soldier tribute with a plaque under it. I found your name on it and I cried. I sat there for like two hours. It was like I could feel your presence. I am sure all the SEALS thought I was some crazy woman, lol. I feel close to you here on the island knowing that you walked some of the same beaches I do and ate at some of the same restaurants I do. I ate some Chinese food the other day and imagined you eating with me since that is one of our favorite foods. (my eyes were watering now, but with more joy than pain. She was becoming the woman I knew she would, and it was gratifying to see.) Blaine and I will be getting a place soon and he says he wants to be in politics. I roll my eyes every time he says it, but I do believe that he will make a great senator someday. He has the gift of gab and people are drawn to him. We will see how that goes. I hope wherever you are that you watch out for me. I need your protection and imagine you with me all the time. I will be taking my Lieutenant JG exam soon and soon after that the lieutenant exam; then I will be the same rank as you when you were in. After that, you will have to salute me, lol. I hope you can read these because I enjoy talking to you this way. I keep your picture with me and think about you all the time. I know it seems I am rambling on, but I just wanted to say hello again. I will write to you again soon. Be careful with whatever you are doing now. I miss and love you so much.

~Gesa

P.S. By the way.................I am Pregnant!

"IN MEMORY OF JACOB"

Romans 8:38–39

For I am convinced that neither death nor life, neither angels nor demons, neither the present nor the future, nor any powers, neither height nor depth, nor anything else in all creation, will be able to separate us from the love of God that is in Christ Jesus our Lord.

National Suicide Hotline
1–800–273–8255
www.suicidepreventionlifeline.org